## A CANDLELIGHT ECSTASY ROMANCE

*"You silly little fool,"* he muttered affectionately.

His lips brushed hers in a gentle salute, so swift and light she might have imagined it. She wished he would wrap her more tightly in his arms, hold her with more than fondness. She wished he would crush her close to him, kiss her with passion and touch her with desire.

Recognition dawned with the shattering force of an explosion behind her closed eyelids.

"I love him," she silently admitted to herself, and knew the bitter taste of her own despair.

Dear Reader:

In response to your enthusiam for Candlelight Ecstasy Romances, we are now increasing the number of titles per month from two to three.

We are pleased to offer you sensuous novels set in America depicting modern American women and men as they confront the provocative problems of a modern relationship.

Throughout the history of the Candlelight line, Dell has tried to maintain a high standard of excellence, to give you the finest in reading pleasure. It is now and will remain our most ardent ambition.

Vivian Stephens
Editor
Candlelight Romances

# The Heart's Awakening

## Rose Marie Ferris

*A CANDLELIGHT ECSTASY ROMANCE*

Published by
Dell Publishing Co., Inc.
1 Dag Hammarskjold Plaza
New York, New York 10017

Dell ® TM 681510, Dell Publishing Co., Inc.

ISBN: 0-440-13519-2

Printed in the United States of America

First printing—June 1981

## Chapter One

It was seeing the photographs that finally reduced Eden to tears. Long before, when she was only a child, she had vowed that she would never cry again. Now, on the occasion of the death of a dear friend, the vow was involuntarily broken.

Annie Holmes had been more of a mother to Eden Lange than her natural mother had been. When Eden's parents had gone their separate ways after a brief, stormy marriage, her mother had been awarded custody of Eden's twin sister, Elaine, while Eden had remained in her father's care. The small house Jonathan Lange and his wife had shared was sold, as were most of their joint belongings, and the modest proceeds were equally divided between them. Florence Lange took Elaine and returned to live with her older brother, Frank Eden, and his wife, Justine.

Jonathan had married late in life, and despite the many arguments he and Flo had had, despite the outright turbulence of their relationship, his wife and twin daughters had been the very center of his existence. He was shaken and bewildered by the breakup of his marriage, by the breakup of his home.

Annie had become the mainstay in the lives of Jonathan and his infant daughter. She'd taken care of Eden, filling the gap as both mother and father until Jonathan roused himself, at least partially, from his grief.

They'd moved into rooms in her boardinghouse—a drafty, three-story, steamboat Gothic monstrosity that perched on a promontory overlooking Humboldt Bay. The house was totally unprotected by trees or by any kind of barrier to soften the blast of the prevailing ocean winds that howled around it and through it, so that it had long since developed a noticeable list to the southeast and seemed in imminent danger of sliding down the hill. Its splintery fish-scale shingles bore only traces of the different colors of paint that had once graced the house, for, as Annie had once remarked to Eden, trying to keep it painted would be like painting the Golden Gate Bridge. It was true enough that paint was stripped from the siding by the wind and rain almost as quickly as it was applied, and years ago Annie had given up spending the time and money that were required to maintain the place.

Dilapidated and unsightly though it was, Eden

loved the house. Until she was almost ten years old, it had been home to her.

Now it was the day after Annie's funeral and, since she'd had no known relatives, the task of sorting through Annie's personal effects had fallen to Eden. She had already finished crating most of Annie's clothing and was congratulating herself on her stoicism when she found the box of photographs pushed far to the back of the shelf in the bedroom closet. It was concealed behind musty World War II-style hats; handbags so ancient, their "genuine imitation" leather was cracked; and several pairs of mildewed, spike-heeled shoes with curled-up toes.

Of these vintage articles Eden salvaged only the hats. They were in fairly good condition, and the way styles changed, they might well be the height of fashion in the fall. She'd set them aside to be added to the carton that was destined for delivery to the thrift shop and was poking around blindly in the darkest reaches of the corner in order to make sure she had emptied it when she felt the cardboard shoe box.

She stretched as far as she was able, but she could reach it only with the very tips of her fingers. She was trying to pull it toward her with the hook of a wire coat hanger when she tipped it off the shelf, and the pictures it contained spilled out, landing in an untidy heap on the closet floor.

Some of the snapshots were of an era so long ago, they were faded and brittle. Eden replaced them in the box with cautious respect for their age but with only a cursory glance at each. She recognized none of the people in the pictures, and there was nothing written on them to offer a clue as to who the proud owner of the new LaSalle was or who the individuals were in the family group that evidently comprised five generations.

She found one photo that she examined more closely before setting it aside to keep for herself, recognizing one of the subjects as a much younger Annie. Pompadoured and dressed in the short-skirted, broad-shouldered style of the early forties, Annie was posed smiling into the eyes of a young man in a navy uniform as they stood with their arms about each other's waists.

*I wonder who he was,* Eden mused. Annie had never mentioned having had a sweetheart. She looked at the picture a second time and realized that as a young woman, Annie Holmes had possessed a high-spirited, vivacious attractiveness far removed from the blowsy, phlegmatic older woman Eden had known and loved.

She had replaced almost all of the pictures when she found the series taken of herself, Jonathan, and Annie. There were nine of them: one made on the occasion of each of her birthdays from age one to nine. She arranged them in chronological order and saw herself grow from a chubby, angelic one-year-old to a leggy, sassy nine; saw Annie become grayer and more slatternly, while Jonathan grew thinner and more haggard with each passing year.

An impractical dreamer, Annie had called him. Others less kind had branded him a fool. But to Eden he'd been extravagantly affectionate, humorous, patient, often absent-minded, yet infinitely wise. He'd been the one reliable purveyor of information who was always willing and able to answer satisfactorily all of the endless questions so important to a child.

Florence Lange and her brother had condemned him because he'd been unable to provide more than the bare necessities for his daughter. They had never recognized the rare, unselfish gift of love he had bestowed on Eden.

He had died of leukemia shortly before Eden's tenth birthday, and she'd been summarily uprooted. She had been removed from the colorfully relaxed ambience of Annie's boardinghouse and transplanted to the hothouse atmosphere of Frank and Justine's home, where she was reunited with her mother and sister.

Until that time, Eden had known only her father's gentle, unceasing consideration for the feelings and rights of others; his and Annie's benign neglect had permitted her the freedom and space to explore and expand her own interests and potentials. She'd been stunned by her aunt and uncle's callous disparagement in the manner of her upbringing and by the pettiness of their carping criticism of Jonathan.

On one occasion she had tried to run away and she'd made her way across town to Annie's house. By the time she arrived, she was burning with resentment. She'd given up weeping and swore nothing would ever make her cry again.

When she'd asked Annie why her relatives hated

her father so, Annie explained calmly and with—for her—surprising eloquence. "They're jealous, Kitten. The only thing Jonathan was guilty of was having a poetic view of life and a pure soul. He wasn't capable of judging anyone harshly, let alone hating them. His way of life was a reminder to Frank and Justine— even to Flo—of their own worst failings as human beings, and that's why they're so intolerant of him."

Although at the time, Eden had been too young to completely understand Annie's logic, she had been comforted by it. Remembering it now, aware of the moisture left by tears on her cheeks, she was consoled again as she transferred these personal mementos to her handbag for safekeeping. Later tonight, she promised herself, she would spend as long as she liked looking at them.

In the last few years there had been a resurgence of interest in the poetry of Jonathan Lange, and within a select academic circle his works were attaining ever higher levels of renown. There had been a number of articles about him in popular national magazines, and many of the local residents had dredged up a favorite anecdote or two they could recite to illustrate how close a personal friend they had been to him. He'd become something of a legend to the townspeople.

The irony inherent in the fact that Elaine had only lately discovered that Jonathan had not been entirely bereft of laudable traits was not lost on Eden. She pitied her sister for her inability to appreciate their father *because* of his many fine qualities rather than blindly following the lead of others who said these qualities were to be admired.

The imperious ring of the telephone came as a jarring intrusion into Eden's musings, and it was with no small effort that she answered it in a cool, businesslike tone.

"Eden? How are you, dear?"

It was Elaine, and the cloying sweetness of the false concern in her voice caused Eden to reply flippantly, with silent apologies to Annie's memory: "Sorry to disappoint you, but I'm fine."

"Oh . . ." Elaine sounded taken aback. "Well, that's good, because Jerry and I would like you to have dinner with us this evening."

"I'd be happy to oblige, Elaine, but I've given my official food-taster the day off."

There was a gasp from the other end of the line before Elaine spoke again, tearfully petulant.

"How *could* you, Eden? It's hateful of you to insinuate that Jerry and I would want to harm you in any way when we only want to help."

"Of course, I should have guessed. You've both been so helpful since I came home," Eden remarked breezily. "I have no reason to question your motives in inviting me to your home after—is it three months since I've returned? How time does fly when you're having fun!" Her voice was tinged with bitterness as she exclaimed, "My God, Elaine, you haven't even bothered to return my telephone calls for the past two months!"

"Eden, please try to understand." Elaine was

cajoling now. "I know Jerry and I should have behaved very differently toward you. We both realize that now. We were so sorry to hear about Annie's death and—well, you're not going to be able to stay on at her place now, and we know you haven't been able to find a job—"

"Naturally you'd know, Elaine," Eden interrupted tartly, "when it's your devoted husband who's had me blacklisted so that no one will employ me."

"Darling, aren't you being a teensy bit paranoid about this? Even if Jerry wanted to 'blacklist' you, as you call it, he hasn't that kind of influence. You might give some thought to the possibility that your rather—shall we say, 'colorful'—reputation has kept you from finding work."

"Oh, there's no question in my mind that my reputation is the indirect reason so many jobs I've applied for have fallen through. Jerry may not be able to throw his weight around personally, but his bank is certainly a very persuasive argument when he chooses to use it on the merchants and businesspeople who depend on it for their line of credit," Eden retorted. "And as to the direct reason . . . well, we all know bankers and their families—right down to their sisters-in-law—like clergymen and Caesar's wife, have to be above reproach. It must be most uncomfortable for Jerry, since my presence here poses such a threat to his image of unswerving integrity." She finished with mock sympathy. "The sanctity of the vault must be protected, I suppose, like some hallowed shrine."

Elaine's gusty sigh told Eden her sister's patience was nearly exhausted.

"The point is, Eden, Jerry has found a job for you, if you still want one."

Eden was speechless with surprise, and when she did not reply, Elaine continued.

"Please, darling, at least say you'll come for dinner and listen with an open mind to Jerry's proposition. You needn't take him up on it unless you want to."

Eden capitulated grudgingly and agreed to be ready when Jerry came to pick her up at seven that evening. Even as she did so, she had the feeling that she might eventually have cause to regret her impulsiveness in accepting the invitation. But what option did she have? She had very little money, no job, and, with the roadblocks Jerry had placed in her path, few expectations of obtaining one. And as Elaine had pointed out, she'd have no place to stay once her chores here were finished and no place to go when she left.

Because they had seen each other very rarely in the nearly ten-year interval immediately after their parents' separation, Eden and Elaine had never been truly close companions. Still, the open hostility that now existed between them was a recent development.

When they were younger, Eden had felt protective toward her sister, whose life in Frank and Justine's home was sheltered in the extreme. There were so many things Elaine was prohibited from doing. The carefree activities of childhood were not for her;

there were few places she was allowed to go without an adult as chaperon. Her pastimes were dictated; her friends were methodically screened and selected for her; and the books she read, the television and movies she watched, were subject to the strictest censorship. She always had to be specklessly groomed, ladylike in behavior, circumspect in demeanor.

When she first came to live with them, her aunt and uncle had tried to treat Eden in the same masterful fashion and she had been overtly mutinous. She was accustomed to having a great deal of freedom, to making many of her own decisions, and the loosely supervised way she had grown up had actually given her good preparation to do so. Jonathan had always believed that the most important quality he could instill in his daughter was a strong sense of values, and Eden's had been quite precociously well developed.

She recognized that Florence, who had also been raised by her much older brother and his wife, was ill-equipped to handle responsibility. She had abdicated her role as Elaine's mother, allowing Justine to usurp her position, and she drifted like flotsam, seeking only her own pleasure as she skimmed over the surface of life.

Eden had worried that Elaine would turn out the same way. She had also been convinced that the time was bound to come when her sister would rebel against the unreasonable restraints imposed upon her—just as Florence had when she'd married Jonathan against her brother's wishes.

At first Eden had been constantly in trouble because of her open refusal to comply with certain of Frank and Justine's restrictive demands. She persisted in choosing her own friends, books, and activities no matter how the two of them threatened, punished, coaxed, or bribed her; eventually they let her go her own way, mouthing predictions of doom and gloom as to what the future held for her. They considered her a hoyden and an ingrate for not appreciating their efforts to restructure her life to conform to their own narrow ideas.

When she was fifteen or so, after several years of an uneasy truce, Frank and Justine found ample cause to punish her once again—only by then it was, more often than not, over things that Elaine had done. Eden was held accountable for the pilferage of money from Justine's purse, for drinking Frank's liquor, for smoking his cigarettes, for the wild impromptu parties Elaine arranged when her aunt and uncle were away from home. Eden silently accepted whatever disciplinary measures were meted out, feeling that if she were to inform on Elaine, they would not believe her and that only by keeping faith with her sister could she ever hope to help her.

As she laid out fresh clothing for the evening and waited for the tub to fill so she could wash away the grime of the day and soak away its tensions, Eden decided it had been inevitable that the showdown with Frank and Justine should have occurred.

The only surprising thing about it was that it hadn't happened sooner, before she'd reached the age of seventeen. She'd sensed that Frank resented the fact that she challenged his authority and was watching and waiting for some excuse, any excuse, to order her to leave his house. She knew that if it hadn't been over the illicit drugs they'd found hidden in her room, it would have been over something else. In all honesty she had to acknowledge that the hoard of narcotics had presented him with a dilly of an opportunity to wash his hands of his obligation to her.

Again Eden had kept her own counsel. She didn't reveal that she hadn't known the drugs were concealed beneath the outgrown clothing in her bureau drawer. She had withstood Frank's verbal abuse mutely, while Justine and Florence wept and wrung their hands and Elaine watched, white-faced with apprehension. When the tirade ended and she was ordered to go to her room and pack her things, Elaine managed to sneak in to see her privately to thank her for her discretion—for accepting the consequences for her actions.

This was the first time Elaine had admitted her own guilt, and Eden was encouraged by that. She responded by saying she was happy enough to be leaving her uncle's house and dispensing with his guardianship.

What she had not foreseen was that Frank would make sure that the reason for her leaving became public knowledge. Annie had, however.

"Your uncle is a man who's puffed up with false pride, Eden," she had warned. "He's got to play the martyr and spread the word about why you've left or look like a louse for having kicked you out. The way news travels in this town, you won't have much chance of keeping a job. You'd best leave the area for a time until this blows over."

They had talked far into the night until finally, reluctantly, Eden had conceded the practicality of Annie's advice. She had left the small northern California coastal town of Eureka for Santa Rosa the next day.

The five years of her exile passed quickly and pleasantly enough. She'd found work easily and made new friends. She managed to finish high school and after this she took a job as a mother's helper with a family in San Francisco so that she could enroll in college there.

The Schuylers had been very good to her, had never complained about rearranging her work schedule so that she could attend classes. She had effortlessly fitted into their household and was a marvelously easygoing companion for their children, Eunice and Peter junior.

They had grown quite fond of one another. They admired Eden's élan, her determination, and she admired them for being so generous, so willing to give of themselves. Once she told them that theirs was the only basically happy marriage she'd ever encountered and confided that most of the marriages she had observed firsthand had been more like armed camps than true partnerships. This was certainly the case in the two with which she was most intimately acquainted—those of her parents and her aunt and uncle.

It became apparent to Peter and Beverly Schuyler that Eden viewed marriage as a trap to be avoided at all costs, and they were dismayed to discover she harbored this deeply ingrained streak of cynicism. It was certainly at odds with her soft-spoken manner and with her delicately feminine appearance.

However, it explained her elusiveness when any of the young men of her acquaintance tried to become more than a friend to her. She adroitly avoided the least possibility of romantic involvement.

Despite their minor differences, her life with the Schuylers remained one of contentment until she had her accident. It had happened during the rush hour. She'd been on her way home, waiting for a bus on a busy corner in downtown San Francisco, when a child darted into the heavily trafficked street. Reacting instinctively, Eden rushed after him. She recalled a car bearing down on her as she tugged him toward the safety of the curb—then nothing until she regained consciousness in the hospital.

Her first concern was for the child. She was informed he was a four-year-old boy who had suffered no ill effects from the incident but who had acquired a healthy respect for the busy streets of the city. His grateful parents kept vigil at the hospital along with the Schuylers, praying for Eden's full recovery.

For Eden the accident resulted in a head injury

that required surgery to relieve the pressure from a subdural hemorrhage. Her nurse had all but wept when she told her they'd had to cut off Eden's long auburn hair and shave her head to prepare her for the operation.

She was hospitalized for several weeks, and when she was discharged, her doctor advised against returning to her routine of work and school for an additional two or three months. Because she was still so weak, and subject to blinding headaches, Eden didn't argue with him.

The sojourn in the hospital had given her plenty of time to think, and since she had no money and—for the time being—could not work for her keep with the Schuylers, she elected to return to Eureka.

Eden had kept up a correspondence with Annie and knew she'd be welcome to stay with her while she was recuperating. She also knew that Elaine had been married the previous summer to Jerry Reece. Perhaps, safely removed from her uncle's domination, Elaine might also offer her assistance until Eden was strong enough to resume working.

She had always recognized that she would never know a secure sense of inner peace unless she rectified the mistaken impression that people in her hometown had of her. It was not that she was that fond of Eureka, but she was, after all, her father's daughter and she respected his memory too much to want to tarnish it by permitting her own reputation to be sullied unjustly.

With a hurried movement that showed her impatience with herself for ever having believed she could single-handedly fight public opinion, Eden pulled the stopper from the bath. God, what a fool she'd been!

The ancient pipes groaned and gurgled in ominous protest as the water drained from the tub, putting an end to her introspection.

## *Chapter Two*

Jeremy Reece was an ascetic-looking man in his mid-thirties. He had fine, even features, a prim mouth, and hair so neatly dressed that the toothmarks of his comb showed, creating the illusion that his hair had been painted on his scalp. He was myopic and wore wire-rimmed glasses. His style of dress was conservative to a fault—somber three-piece suits, worn with the requisite sincere necktie. Eden had never seen him without the full banker's uniform and doubted that he ever dressed informally.

Despite having dawdled so long in her bath, she was ready and waiting for him when his car pulled in at the front of Annie's house.

Eden dreaded being alone with her brother-in-law, and in order to avoid a lengthy private interview with him, she hastily grabbed the velvet blazer that matched her skirt, retrieved her handbag from the hall table, and nearly ran down the walk to meet him before he'd stopped the engine.

"Eden." Jerry inclined his head toward her as, without waiting for his assistance, she opened the door and climbed in on the passenger side. "Still as impulsive as ever, I see."

Matching him for coolness, she inclined her head in a mocking imitation of his own gesture but did not otherwise respond. She had thought he might say something about the job Elaine had mentioned and when he didn't, she thought, *I'll be damned if I'll give him the impression I'm begging by asking him about it.*

As a consequence, the drive through the town was accomplished in strained silence.

It was early June, and as the sun tumbled toward the horizon the shadows lengthened, throwing objects into sharp relief. Except for the redwoods the only trees in Eureka were ornamental varieties. In this region, where the sun was often shrouded by the Pacific coastal fog, no one did anything to diminish its cheerfulness on the days when it shone clear. Those days were so few that when they occurred, everyone smiled as they commented on what a glorious day it was and savored the warmth and joy of the sunshine.

The rhododendrons and azaleas were putting on their annual display of blossoms in myriad shades of white, pink, lavender, and red. Later in the summer the begonias, cinerarias, nasturtiums, and pelargoniums would bloom. The ice plants would cover the sandy slopes with carpets of fuchsia and red, and the heather and Scotch broom would march through the rich green pastures on the hillsides. The colors of the flowers would remain vibrantly unfaded because of the seemingly ever-present fog, as though nature sought to compensate for the rarity of sunshine with their brilliance.

They passed through an older residential neighborhood, and Eden noticed with aesthetic appreciation the imaginative way in which the Victorian homes that lined the streets had been renovated.

Eureka really hadn't changed much in the five years she'd been away. Not that she'd expected it would have. It was so out-of-the-way, a kind of quiet backwater on the coast midway between San Francisco, hundreds of miles to the south, and Portland, equally far away to the north.

Jerry finally spoke as they turned into the driveway of his and Elaine's house. His voice was stiff with disapproval.

"Elaine told me something of your conversation on the telephone today, and I just want to express my sincere regret that you received the wrong impression from my earlier attempt to help you."

He negated the sentiment to which he'd just paid lip service with his rather constipated smile. He did not look regretful at all, but pained.

"Perhaps it's you who've labored under the wrong impression, Jerry," Eden countered softly. "You see,

I want to stay in Eureka, and you offered me money if I'd leave."

She helped herself out of the car and started to walk unhurriedly toward the house. Jerry caught up with her at the shallow steps to the entryway and detained her with one hand on her arm.

"Please, Eden." His throat worked with apparent agitation. Such an outward sign of emotion in Jerry was tantamount to hysterics in someone else, and she realized how much this meant to him.

"You must consider the fact that you didn't help your cause with the stories you told Elaine about the dissolute way you've conducted yourself the last few years." He frowned and shook his head reprovingly. "The profligate way you lived in the commune—all those men! I'll admit that I would not allow Elaine to see you or invite you to the house, and finally I felt forced, in all good conscience, to put a stop to your talking on the phone to one another. But it's *me* you have to thank for muzzling Elaine when I discovered she was spreading the ugly tales you'd told her about your wanton behavior. At least, as Elaine suggested, listen with an open mind. This is most important, not only to us personally but to the bank and—quite possibly—to the whole town."

Even as she smarted from it, Eden was forced to admit that there was some justice in Jerry's pompous condemnation of her behavior since she'd been home. Of one thing she was heartily ashamed. Elaine had fantasized that Eden's life since she'd left town had consisted of one long orgy, and at last, disgusted with her sister's obsession, Eden had stopped denying it and by default had allowed Elaine to believe that her perverted ideas were the truth.

Acknowledging that if she ever hoped to see her sister on friendly terms, she must arrive at a more amicable relationship with her brother-in-law, Eden asked, "What's it all about, Jerry?"

"It's a long story," he said. He looked relieved that her mood was cooperative. "Let's discuss it after dinner."

He opened the door and guided her into the foyer, where an elegantly garbed and coiffed Elaine waited with her hands outstretched in counterfeit welcome. She presented an exotic, glamorous appearance in the plum-colored hostess gown she wore, and Eden felt drab and uninteresting by comparison.

Elaine was taller than Eden and almost voluptuous, while Eden was slight. Elaine had inherited their mother's dramatic coloring: Her hair was as dark as midnight, her eyes a clear emerald-green, her complexion creamy pale. The fact that Eden resembled her father had never endeared her to her mother's family, and a familiar self-consciousness swept over her as Elaine took Eden's hands in her own, leaned forward, and kissed the air in the vicinity of her cheek.

"Darling," she gushed, "it's so good to see you after all this time! You're looking very . . . healthy."

She gasped as she took note of Eden's shorn head. Her once waist-length hair was only long enough now to riot in a cloud of downy soft, wispy curls that hugged her finely modeled head.

"But your beautiful hair," Elaine sympathized. "Oh, what a shame!"

Eden smiled ruefully and quipped, "As a hair stylist, my barber was a good surgeon."

Suddenly perceiving beneath the hostess facade the hint of vulnerability she had always associated with her sister, Eden hugged her with real warmth and volunteered, "I've missed you, Elaine."

Elaine drew back stiffly and smiled. "Well, of course, darling. We *are* twins, after all—the other half of one another."

"We're fraternal, not identical," Eden corrected dryly.

Elaine turned a blank look on her, drew Eden's arm through hers, and patted her hand.

"I'm sure you'd like to freshen up before Alex arrives. You remember Alex Lassiter, don't you? He's joining us for dinner. Come, I'll show you where the powder room is."

The urgency of her manner made Eden feel as though she had a smudge on her nose or had forgotten to wash behind her ears, but she followed docilely enough as Elaine led her to the guest bathroom.

She was obediently washing her hands before her sister's remark about Alex Lassiter sank in. She remembered him. His mother and he had lived next door to Frank and Justine, though by the time she came to stay with them, he'd been away at college most of the year. She'd known his mother better than him.

Paula Lassiter had been the one bright spot in the years she'd spent as her uncle's ward. She'd opened her home and her heart to Eden and, as children will, Eden had sometimes wished that Paula was really her mother.

Alex, she thought. Who could forget him? Tall, dark, and macho. Also sexy. Also brainy. Always surrounded by girls—by women. A new favorite emerging with such predictable regularity, you could almost set your clocks by it.

She made a face at her image in the mirror. She was pale. Her delicate coloring was washed out by the unflattering fluorescent lighting over the vanity so that the sprinkling of freckles across her small, pert nose stood out starkly against the whiteness of her skin. Her gray-blue eyes, fringed with long gold-tipped lashes, had a haunted look about them that hinted of her earlier tears. That would never do.

She rehearsed a smile, broadening it fiercely until a deep dimple appeared in one cheek.

Alex Lassiter, she mused, as her bogus smile faded. He was quite a lot to live up to, even as a dinner partner.

Momentarily she was apprehensive, then she gave herself a mental shake. By now he might have a paunch, a head as bald as a billiard ball, fallen arches, and bad breath.

When she emerged from the powder room, Eden

discovered he was still tall, dark, and sexy, which was not surprising, since he was only thirty or thirty-one. There was not an ounce of superfluous flesh on his broad-shouldered, lean-hipped frame, and his hair was as thick and glossy as ever. The effect of his crooked grin was devastating as he walked toward her, long-legged and lithe.

"This can't be the Munchkin!" he exclaimed as Eden's hand was swallowed in the grasp of his much larger one.

"I'd forgotten you used to call me that—" She paused briefly and added, "Among other things."

She returned his smile but disengaged her hand.

"Sorry about that," Alex said, "but you did make a giant-size pest of your small self at times. I'd get my courage all worked up to kiss my girl and there you were—peering at us through the bushes!"

They laughed easily together, Jerry and Elaine joining in.

"It's I who should apologize," Eden demurred. "As I recall, I was conducting a survey as to how many girls there were and trying to predict how long each one would last." Her smile turned impish. "You were better entertainment than the television shows Uncle Frank would let us watch."

"Somehow I doubt that's a commendation," Alex declared dryly.

Eden shrugged noncommittally and turned to accept a glass of white wine from Jerry.

"What happened to your abundant red hair?" Alex surveyed her shining Titian nimbus of curls.

"She suffered a head injury and they had to cut her hair for surgery," Elaine intervened. "Eden says," she continued, fibbing slyly, "she was injured when she fell off a bar stool!"

Elaine's brittle laughter rippled out, sharp as broken glass, and Eden willed herself to return Alex's questioning glance without changing expression. She hoped she looked bored.

During dinner Elaine drank too much wine, flirted outrageously with Alex, and manufactured the flimsiest excuses to touch him. Her slender graceful fingers trailed along his arm, lingered on his hand and, on at least one occasion, on his thigh. Eden began to wonder whether Annie had been right when she'd conjectured that Elaine had married Jeremy Reece simply to escape her uncle's influence.

To his credit Alex did not encourage Elaine's attentions, but by the time the meal was over, Jerry was steaming with jealousy, Eden surmised, from the way he was perspiring and continually blotting his brow with his spotless handkerchief. Trust Jerry to sweat neatly, she told herself. From time to time he glanced sulkily at Eden, as though it were her doing that Elaine was making such a fool of herself.

It came as a relief when Jerry finally pushed his chair away from the table and suggested they adjourn to the study, excluding Elaine by saying, "We'll excuse you, dear. You'd only find it tedious to have to listen to us discussing business."

When they were settled in the study, Jerry inquired, "What may I get you to drink? A liqueur? Cognac?"

Alex accepted a brandy and Eden declined the offer.

"Abstemious this evening, aren't you," Jerry observed sarcastically.

She had not even finished the wine she'd been served before dinner. She did not care for the taste of alcoholic beverages.

"I'm on the wagon," she said mildly, "and if you hope to convince me to take this job, whatever it is, you're going about it the wrong way."

"Sorry," he muttered. "I'll endeavor to remain businesslike if you will."

Alex watched the exchange with obvious distaste.

"Would you prefer that I explain it to her?" he asked. His voice held the firmness of command.

"By all means," Jerry acceded as he subsided into the swivel chair behind his desk. Selecting a pencil from the holder there, he began doodling on a notepad as though he'd lost interest in the proceedings.

Alex leaned toward Eden, his elbows on his knees, his hands clasped loosely. His dark eyes were intent as they rested on her.

"What's involved is a kind of scientific study that's to be conducted by the Van Damme Foundation during this summer. From mid-June to mid-September a total of thirty couples will be living in remote rural settings in as near isolation as can be achieved. The Foundation hopes there will be minimal contact, either direct or indirect, with other people during that time."

Eden listened with growing fascination as Alex continued.

"The individual partners in each of these couples are to keep a diary and record daily their activities, their thoughts and feelings, details concerning their interaction with their partners; in fact, any occurrence that seems relevant to them. Eventually the data from the diaries will be entered in the computer at the Foundation, collated, and analyzed to see if there are any common denominators to the experiences and reactions of the people involved."

Still maintaining his observation of Eden, Alex sat back in his chair and sipped his brandy.

"The purpose of this study is to increase our fund of knowledge about the effects of isolation on various types of people. The Foundation adhered to a painstaking selection process in assigning the partners involved in an attempt to get a cross section suitable for a statistical sample and everything seemed all set to go until a few days ago when the couple chosen for this area advised us they have to drop out of the project." He smiled briefly.

"It seems the young woman is pregnant, and her doctor advises against her participation."

Eden found she was holding her breath as Alex concluded. "We'd like you, Red, to agree to become the distaff partner in the couple that will be replacing them."

He drained the brandy snifter. "I'll be the other half of the partnership."

She expelled her breath in a long sigh.

"Why me?" she queried flatly.

"You're the right age, sex, and race, and you meet the geographic and demographic requisites. You have other qualities of personality and character that are deemed necessary in this instance."

"Would I be paid for taking part?"

"We'd hardly expect you to participate for the love of it."

He threw a quick smile in her direction.

"There will be a period of debriefing as well, so you'd be expected to hold yourself available until the middle of October."

Eden felt as though her head was whirling with confusion. She wished now she had accepted a drink, that she smoked—anything to offer distraction. Instead, she ran her fingers nervously along the arm of the chair, willing herself to relax and think clearly.

"You said this was important to you personally, Jerry. Why?" she asked.

He looked embarrassed. "Couldn't we hash that out later?"

Alex moved his hand impatiently in a short, chopping motion.

"I believe Jerry was referring to the fact that the Van Damme Foundation is considering establishing a research center in northern California. They're doing feasibility studies in Eureka as well as several other locations. Jerry hopes they'll elect to go ahead with the site here if they receive ample cooperation in carrying out this project. Naturally, as head of the commercial loans department in one of the local banks, he would benefit from this decision. It could profit the entire area, actually, since such facilities are an enormous attraction for many types of industrial operations."

"Will my cooperation, or lack of it, make any difference in whether the ultimate decision is favorable to Eureka?"

"That's impossible for me to say. Obviously Jerry believes that it might."

"There's nothing unethical—" Eden began and Jerry interrupted brusquely.

"No. You can be assured of that."

"It sounds very intriguing, but why do I get the feeling you haven't told me everything?" Eden looked directly at Alex as she posed this question.

"Maybe because I haven't. There are quite a few specifics we haven't covered. If you agree, you'll be issued a manual that will help you to prepare for the project."

Unexpectedly he smiled. "But I think what you're asking is whether there is any kind of catch, and there is one. If you agree to do this, we'd have to be married." His expression was inscrutable as he continued. "It's merely a formality—a legal technicality. We'd have the marriage annulled at the end of the summer."

"Why is it necessary, then?" Eden asked tensely.

"It's simply a nuisance condition imposed by Milton Graham, the director of the project, that all the couples engaged in the study must be married. There's no scientific necessity for it, but Milt is an elderly man and tends to be straitlaced in his attitudes toward certain things. Chief among these is sexual permissiveness. So you see, what it boils down to is that it's a matter of not offending his sensibilities."

Alex studied her with narrowed eyes as though gauging her reaction as he finished his explanation. Eden attempted to remain impassive, to hide her inner turmoil behind a blank exterior. Before she could formulate an adequate response, Jerry interceded.

"Eden, before you reach a decision, consider the fact that the main issue at stake as far as you are concerned is improving your reputation, especially at this time, when people here are just beginning to give you the benefit of the doubt again."

He smiled smugly at her as he leaned back in his chair. "Your father is on the threshold of becoming a local folk hero. I'm sure you wouldn't want to do anything further that might reflect badly on his memory. Furthermore," he continued, "if you still want to remain in the area at the end of the summer, I'll remove my opposition. I'll even help you to find a job."

She felt her face grow warm with embarrassment as Jerry advanced his argument. She realized she had underestimated him badly. He was more perceptive than she'd thought, but she was determined not to show that he had successfully disconcerted her and forced herself to lift her chin proudly and smile.

"I shudder to think what will happen to my reputation when it becomes public knowledge that I've lived with a man in isolated splendor—in the state of holy wedlock—for three months, only to have the marriage annulled on grounds of nonconsummation."

Jerry looked as though he'd like to strangle her, and the pencil he was holding snapped between his suddenly taut fingers.

"Will you never be serious, Eden?" he spluttered.

"Take it easy, Jerry." Alex grinned at her. "I think Red has a valid point. I wouldn't be too happy over such a unique set of circumstances becoming widely known either."

On that friendly note he glanced at his watch and got to his feet.

"I'm late for another appointment, so I must be going now," he announced as he crossed the few paces that divided him from Eden, his hand extended.

When he clasped her hand in farewell, she was overwhelmingly aware of the warm strength of his fingers, the tensile power contained in his lean, athletic body.

"You'd probably like to think about this before you reach a decision," he suggested softly.

His dark eyes captured her smoky gray ones, smiling boldly, speaking silently.

Aloud he said, "I'm sorry to have to rush you, but I must have your answer by tomorrow."

She wanted to shout "No! I won't do it," but as he released her hand the touch of his fingertips gliding lightly across her palm was like a lazy caress, and her eyes widened with surprise that such a casual gesture could be so terribly intimate. She was shaking inside, but her voice was steady as she heard herself agreeing that she would let him know the following morning what she had decided.

As he went with Jerry to the door of the study, Eden called after him hopefully, "I don't suppose you have fallen arches."

Alex turned back toward her abruptly, bemused by the impertinence of the question but not offended.

"No," he answered gravely, "I don't suppose I do."

## Chapter Three

From her vantage point on the porch of Annie's house, Eden could see beyond the mouth of the bay that was formed by the narrow jaws of the sand spits and rocky jetties, to the point where the dark cobalt of the ocean blended into the lighter blue of the sky. Closer in, on the mudflats of the south bay, a few clam diggers scurried about, pausing occasionally to excavate for their quarry.

An oceanbound fishing trawler chugged across the bar, rising and falling on the smoothly rolling swells of the gentle waves in the channel. She watched it as it threaded its way through the strait, imitating the rhythm of its rise and fall with the motion of the porch swing. Her concentration was so complete that she was unaware of Alex's approach until he sat beside her in the glider.

"Sorry if I startled you," he said, noticing her wide-eyed look of alarm. "I called good morning to you, but you were worlds away."

She returned to her intent observation of the fishing boat without replying to his comment.

The rusted springs of the glider creaked a strident accompaniment to its motion, weaving an oddly hypnotic spell.

The morning was clear and cool, and the playful breezes—not unpleasantly scented with a blend of salt and fish and iodine—ruffled Eden's hair, tossing it into a silky disorder so that her coppery curls, shiny and bright as a newly minted penny, framed her face like the petals of a flower. She sensed Alex's dark-eyed gaze on her face as acutely as if he'd physically stroked it and forced her eyes to meet his as she ventured, "I was just thinking that if I were to watch that trawler down there until it disappeared beyond the rim of the horizon, it would still exist. Even though we could no longer see it, it would still exist." She closed her eyes and rested her head wearily against the upright that supported the canopy of the swing. "And it occurred to me that maybe that's what death is also—a kind of parallel existence on another plane, in a new dimension."

Alex touched her hand sympathetically.

"I was sorry to hear about Annie Holmes," he said. "She was a truly remarkable woman."

Her eyes flew open momentarily then slowly closed again when she saw he was not being condescending.

"What's going to become of this place now?"

"It's been declared structurally unsound and it's to be dismantled. A local developer has contracted to tear it down for the salvage value of some of the woodwork and fixtures, and the authorities are trying to locate Annie's closest surviving relatives. If they don't find anyone eligible to inherit, I'm not sure what will happen to the proceeds, but I suppose they'll go to the state."

Her voice was unsteady as she revealed more. "Annie died without having made a will. It was so sudden, you see. She seemed fine when she went to bed the night she died. She just—didn't wake up the next morning."

Tears welled hotly behind her closed eyelids, and she squeezed them tightly together to keep the tears from falling. "It's strange to think of the chandeliers and windows becoming part of the decor of a seafood restaurant," she said in a choked voice.

She was aware of Alex's weight shifting slightly in the swing and heard him strike a match before the aroma of his pipe tobacco reached her. He smoked in silence for a time, giving her the opportunity to regain her composure before he asked, "Have you reached a decision?"

"Not one I'm comfortable with. I'd like to participate in the study. It's really a very tempting offer." Eden sighed, rose restlessly, and walked to the porch railing, where she looked toward the ocean again. She crossed her arms protectively over her breasts, her hands rubbing her bare arms to warm them as the freshening wind chilled them.

"But—" Alex prompted.

"It's the marriage thing," she blurted adamantly. "I—I just can't envision going through with that in order to take part in the study."

She wheeled to face Alex, sensing the reassurance he was about to offer.

"Oh, I understand it's to be only a formality, but I guess it's a phobia with me or something. Just thinking about it makes me feel spooked."

He stood and came to join her by the railing, smiling as he touched her cheek lightly.

"You're a funny little thing," he remarked.

Her eyes flashed irately and she pulled sharply away from his touch.

"I meant funny as in strange, inconsistent—not funny ha-ha."

"I aim to please," she said stiffly.

"And you do, in more ways than you realize." His eyes crinkled with good humor as his grin broadened. "Still, you're something of a Chinese puzzle, and I'd like to know what the combination is that will make you open up."

"What makes you think I'm not open?"

His expression clearly showed his deep amusement with her, and he shook his head.

"Oh, lady, if you only knew!" he exclaimed dryly. "Little things give you away, but if you want a more specific answer than that, I'll refuse to oblige you by giving it to you. I have no desire to aid you in perfecting this ridiculous role you assume."

In a reflexive action of outrage her hand swung in a swift arc toward his face, but, with lightning grace, he caught her wrist in a viselike grip and, pulling her toward him, he forced her arms behind her back and held her securely while she fought ineffectually to break free. She tried to kick him, and he easily quelled her attempts, locking her more tightly within his grasp so that, through the heat of her anger, she became uncomfortably aware of their closeness. Against her will, her senses responded with unwonted intensity to the pressure of his muscular thighs that imprisoned her against the railing, to the hardness of his chest almost painfully crushing her breasts. She damned her own softness and relative weakness as she gasped for breath, spent and exhausted from the uneven struggle.

"Let me go," she implored him, hating the pleading note in her voice, hating him for being the cause of it.

"When you calm down," he replied evenly. He wasn't even winded.

He eased his hold on her slightly, and she gulped deep drafts of air, willing herself to relax. He released her arms, and she stood quiescent as his hands moved to her waist. He held her loosely, his chin resting against the top of her head, until the last of the tension drained from her, and she was pliant in his arms.

"Have you learned anything from this experience, Red?" His manner was detached and clinical.

"Yes," she replied tonelessly. "I've learned that because you're bigger and stronger than I am, you assume you can say anything you want to about me."

His hands tightened in punishment about her waist.

"What about you, you acid-tongued little hellcat? Do you think you don't trade on your fragile femininity? If another man had taken a swing at me as you just did, I certainly wouldn't have reacted by holding him in my arms to subdue him!"

He gave her a little shake before he continued, and she did not offer resistance.

"I've demonstrated something else though, and if you'll consider it objectively, it may help you to overcome your anxiety about our pseudomarriage."

Eden looked up at him incredulously.

"As you pointed out, I am bigger and stronger than you, but I've taken no sexual liberties."

His hands fell away from her to rest on his narrow hips as he stepped back, and she clutched at the railing behind her for support as he surveyed her. His eyes traveled with slow insolence over her body before they rose to her face.

"You're not my type, Red," he said analytically. "I think you'd be a stimulating companion intellectually, but physically you leave me cold! So stop being foolish and say you'll take part in the project. You know you want to."

Cursing herself for her weakness, for her treachery, she complied with his suggestion.

Once, when she was old enough to see the way her father still cared for her mother, the way he yearned for her in spite of the contemptuous way she treated him, Eden had innocently asked, "Why do you love her, Daddy?"

At a loss for words Jonathan had replied after a long silence, "Because I have no other choice."

The choked tone of his voice revealed his torment, and Eden was frightened. The anguished, unseeing expression in her father's eyes made him seem a stranger.

"Do you love her better than me?" she demanded, childishly trying to monopolize his attention.

"I love her differently." He sighed deeply. "You're my daughter, and the love I feel for you is the love of helping to create and mold a new person. It's love of the promise in you for the future. It's the hope of immortality."

He smiled and for a moment she was reassured. Then he continued.

"The feeling I have for your mother is the love of a man for a woman, and that kind of love can cause joy or pain, sweetness or bitterness, solace or despair —strength or weakness."

As he'd spoken, his face had become shuttered. Her father retreated behind a mask of pain, and the stranger was there again.

"When I grow up, I'm never going to love anyone

like that," Eden declared vehemently, wrapping her arms tightly about his neck and hugging him as hard as she could, seeking to console him.

He stroked her hair absently. "Yes, you will, Kitten," he prophesied resignedly. "Someday you'll meet the right man and you'll have no alternative."

She'd felt as if he'd struck her. It seemed that that kind of love had brought him only misery, yet with the words he'd spoken, he'd consigned her to the same fate.

For an instant she'd felt like weeping, almost accepting his forecast for her as having been preordained. Then, setting her small chin with determination, she'd resolved silently, "No! No, I won't. I'll never love a man that way and I'll never get married," for in her child's mind the two were inseparable.

Love and marriage were inseparable in her adult mind as well—and in the years since that conversation with her father, she had seen nothing to change her opinion regarding either abject state. On the contrary she'd witnessed a number of her friends falling in love and marrying. At first every facet of their lives together would be colored by their happiness. Then passion faded and disillusion set in, like so much dry rot, eating away at the fabric of the relationship until there was not even a husk of love remaining. At that point, more often than not, the happiness was cast aside and only the people remained—used up by the emotion.

This was what she had so diligently avoided. Although she dated frequently and had quite a few male friends whose companionship she valued and enjoyed, she ruthlessly severed the friendship if she received a hint of any deeper attraction on either side.

Eden knew that most of her friends would consider ludicrous the fact that, at the age of twenty-two, she was still a virgin—especially when this fact was juxtaposed against the one that her reputation among the people of her hometown was far from chaste. If the Schuylers ever compared notes with Frank and Justine, they'd think she had the nature of a modern-day Jekyll and Hyde.

She smiled grimly to herself at this thought as she tucked a few last-minute items into the backpack she would carry on the hike to the cabin where Alex and she were to spend the summer. She had learned it was located just outside the northern boundary of the national wilderness area in the Marble Mountains and was accessible only to pedestrian traffic. The terrain they would cross to reach it was even too rugged for horses to traverse, although a local supplier had stocked it with food and other necessities for the summer that he had packed in with donkeys. Alex and she would carry in only their own clothing and other personal things.

As she went over her checklist to be certain she had included everything, Eden sighed. In less than an hour now Alex was coming to take her to the courthouse where Judge Kearney was to perform their wedding ceremony. Elaine and Jerry were to be their witnesses and the only guests. It was to be simple, quick, painless, and private, since neither she nor Alex regarded it as anything other than a formality to be observed. Alex had compared it to obtaining a driver's license before one could legally drive a car.

She was reassured to some extent by his dispassionate attitude toward the wedding. He had disclosed the plans for it in the same impersonal way he'd told her about the cabin, briefed her on other details pertaining to the project, and overseen her selection of durable clothing that would be appropriate for the summer.

With all the necessary shopping, the chores connected with winding up Annie's estate, and the extensive medical and psychological testing through which Alex had shepherded her in the past week, she'd been kept too busy to reconsider her decision, but now that she thought about it, her own reactions were more troubling than anything Alex had done. First there had been her deviation from the safe pattern she'd set for herself so long ago when she'd agreed to the imposed condition that they marry. Since then it seemed to her that at times she hardly recognized herself.

Her temperament was usually quite even, and she was not prone to moodiness, yet all too often over the past week she'd wavered between laughter and tears. For no good reason one minute she would be filled with expectation and excitement—as though hovering on the verge of some fantastic discovery—the next she would feel depressed or irritable. Her attention wandered so, that she found it difficult to concentrate and she forgot the most ordinary things.

She had been worried that all this was due to some delayed aftereffect of her concussion, but all the tests she'd had at her physical examination earlier in the week had shown normal results, and the doctor was pleased with the completeness of her recovery. The only symptoms he attributed to her injury were the occasional severe headaches she had. The doctor approved of, even applauded, her plans for the summer.

Putting the list away, Eden wandered through the empty, echoing rooms of Annie's house for one last time. Some of them still held fond associations because of former tenants who had boarded with Annie.

The room that was wallpapered with faded pink cabbage roses she thought of as Miss Tillie Frobisher's. She'd been a retired schoolteacher who'd had a stern, no-nonsense manner and who could fix a mischievous child with a glance that was so all-seeing that when Eden was a little girl, Miss Tillie was the one adult she'd never tried to put anything over on. One look at her and you knew it wasn't worth the effort.

She had held Eden spellbound with her memories of some of the famous and infamous people who had been important to the development of Humboldt County. Because Miss Tillie had been lonely and had already exhausted the interests of the others at the boardinghouse with her long-winded tales, when she found she had a new and willing audience in Eden,

49

a strong bond of affection had formed between the elderly spinster and the little girl.

Just down the hall from Miss Tillie's room was Professor Bellini's. Not for the first time, Eden asked herself, Professor of what? She'd never known, and neither had anyone else. Nor had anyone known what his first name was, so everyone simply called him Professor. Suddenly it occurred to her that maybe that *was* his given name.

He'd been a man of mystery. No one knew what he'd done for a living either, and she was the only one who'd discovered his avocation: He'd constructed driftwood sculptures on the slender crescent of beach between the highway and the bay to the north of town—much to the astonished delight of local residents and tourists. He'd built his structures only in the dead of night so that his works of art seemed to appear magically—an airplane, a windmill, a pirate ship run aground beneath the eucalyptus trees that lined the road. Sometimes he'd taken Eden with him on his forays and she'd served as an accomplice and sculptor's apprentice by beachcombing, tirelessly and enthusiastically, to supply the exact piece of driftwood he required.

No one else had ever discovered who the talented artist was, and soon he'd had impersonators, but none of their works had rivaled the stylized whimsy of the Professor's. Eden found she was smiling at the memory of them as she left his room.

Most of the contents of the house had been sold at auction the previous day and, deserted as it was by its old familiar furniture, it seemed to have lost its power to make her feel at home. She toured the rest of the rooms more quickly.

The one with the stained-glass window, still lovely despite being flyspecked and grimed with soot, had been Ernie Trautman's. He'd owned a tavern and had worn his sorrowful face proudly, like a badge of duty honorably earned through long years of service as a sympathetic listener to his patrons' problems. He'd also proved to have a vast store of pithy advice when, as a small girl, Eden had now and again approached him with her own worries.

Her last stop was the attic bedroom where Lars Nilssen had lived. He'd been a commercial fisherman who had tutored her on the tides and the moon and where it was most rewarding to look for tuna or petrale sole when they were running offshore. It was Lars who had taken her to witness the annual migration of the gray whales when they frolicked along the northern California coast. He had been lost at sea when his boat had gone down during a storm, but she still treasured the blown-glass spheres he'd given her. He'd found them on one of his fishing trips—floats from the nets of Japanese seiners from the other side of the Pacific.

Finally, her good-byes to the house completed, she descended the steep, narrow stairway to the second floor. Returning to her own room, Eden was drawn to the dressing table, where she paused and surveyed her appearance in the mirror.

She hadn't many clothes and she was wearing the

same pearl-gray pleated skirt and velvet blazer, the same dark blue blouse she'd worn for Annie's memorial services and for the dinner at Elaine's. She was appropriately dressed for either a funeral or a business appointment—and in the last analysis she felt she was bound for a combination of the two. She was going to enter into a marriage contract and temporarily bury her freedom.

Her eyes were wide and darkly shadowed. Was it a distortion caused by the slightly wavy surface of the aged looking-glass that made them seem frightened, that made her look as wraithlike and insubstantial as the old friends who lived on only in her memories?

She reached out and traced her reflection with her fingertips. Her hand trembled momentarily before she steadied it, firmly following the outlines of the fine-boned cheeks, the rounded chin, the winglike brows, the tremulous fullness of her mouth with its childishly short upper lip, seeking to prove that the vulnerable young woman she saw in the mirror was not a realistic reproduction of her flesh-and-blood self.

She was seized by an inner trembling that persisted throughout Alex's arrival and their perfunctory exchange of pleasantries and throughout the drive to the courthouse. As they neared Judge Kearney's chambers Eden hung back, and Alex looked down at her quizzically.

"There should be a sign over the door, reading, 'Abandon Hope, All Ye Who Enter Here,' " Eden whispered, speaking more to herself than to him and following her quote with a shaky little laugh.

Alex's dark brows drew together in a frown, and he clamped his arm about her shoulders and propelled her forcefully into the judge's office.

Elaine, Jerry, and the judge were waiting for them. Elaine was radiantly beautiful, and in the lime-green silk shantung dress she was wearing, she looked far more bridelike than Eden. Elaine pressed a bouquet of roses into her hands, and Alex looked slightly embarrassed at the unwanted festive note they added to the occasion.

Jerry wore his usual dark banker's suit and ostentatiously pious expression, while Judge Kearney presented a dignified figure in his robes as he greeted Eden with solemn courtliness.

Alex also wore a light gray suit and a navy blue shirt that was patterned with matching gray. We're twins, Eden thought, successfully controlling a hysterical desire to giggle. Was it a good omen that they wore nearly identical colors? Probably he, too, was mourning the loss of his single blessedness.

She stared up at him as he recited his vows in a deep, resonant monotone. His swarthy, ruggedly handsome face was as expressionless as his voice, and it struck her that he was so unmoved, he might have been reciting the telephone directory. She wondered what it would be like if he were to look at her with love; she imagined his firmly contoured lips softening sensuously to kiss her, and shivered.

Her own voice was barely audible as she repeated

her lines, and when Alex took her hand to slip the narrow gold band onto her finger, he looked faintly surprised, for it was icy in contrast to the heat of his. He continued to hold her hand, warming it until the service ended.

Afterward there were inane offerings of congratulations and Judge Kearney shook her hand vigorously, saying, "Best wishes for every happiness, Mrs. Lassiter."

*My God,* Eden realized with rising panic, *that's me!* She was suddenly confused, uncertain whether to laugh or to cry. More than anything, she wanted to run from the judge's office, and she was grateful for the sureness of Alex's hand at the small of her back as he guided her out of the courthouse and into his car.

He climbed in on the driver's side, lithely folding his big frame into the bucket seat, and sat gripping the wheel, staring out at the fog-blurred street.

Eden studied his hands: long, well-formed, sun-browned, and warm. She was familiar with the strength of them. Could they be gentle as well?

She shivered again and with an impatient gesture Alex tore the carnation Elaine had placed there from his lapel and tossed it derisively onto the backseat of the sedan.

"Well, that's done," he said flatly, and his voice was as cold as Eden felt as she averted her eyes to concentrate on the creamy perfection of the yellow rosebuds she held.

Neither of them spoke during the drive to Alex's

home, where he delivered her, like an unwanted parcel, into his mother's presence before excusing himself to deal with last-minute preparations for their trip into the mountains the following morning.

## Chapter Four

Paula Lassiter was as sweet-natured as ever, in spite of being afflicted with arthritis, which had progressed to the degree that she was now confined to a wheelchair. There were days, Eden knew, when the slightest movement was painful for her, yet she remained smiling, uncomplaining, and youthful in her outlook, although her lovely face was seamed by pain and her dark hair liberally frosted with silver.

"It's good to see you, Eden." Paula welcomed her warmly, offering her soft, fragrant cheek for Eden's kiss. "I'm happy to find you haven't changed too drastically in all the years you've been away. I hoped you would stop in and visit me when I heard you'd come home."

"I'm sorry I didn't before," Eden replied earnestly

as she stirred uneasily in her chair. "I would have if I'd known you'd wanted me to."

"You needn't stand on ceremony with me, my dear," Paula said graciously, putting Eden at ease. "I realize that there are certain people in town who haven't received you as they should have. But let me assure you that I know you too well ever to believe the malicious gossip that's been bandied about concerning your activities."

"If everyone were as generous as you, the world would be a wonderful place," Eden remarked wistfully.

"I'm only sorry I wasn't able to attend the wedding."

Eden was startled by the apology, and Paula continued hurriedly. "Oh, I know all about the reasons for it, and that it's only an interim arrangement." She paused briefly. "I can't say that I approve. I think it's high time my son married for real, you see, and produced some grandchildren for me to spoil. But it was your and Alex's decision, and I wish I'd been able to offer you the support of my being there."

"I appreciate the fact you'd like to have been present. I only wish I'd known before," Eden admitted candidly. "I could have used your moral support."

"I can imagine." Paula laughed merrily. "How well I remember you as a very little girl, proclaiming in your strangely mature way that you'd never marry. You were always so unpredictable, so independent and lively, I never knew what to expect from you next."

"In other words," Eden countered, "I was a brat."

"You had your moments," Paula returned honestly. "But you were much too unspoiled and tenderhearted to be a thoroughgoing brat."

The rattle of china and cutlery heralded the approach of a tall teen-age girl who entered the living room, wheeling a hostess cart that contained a tea tray. She had long, light brown hair and a striking, coltish attractiveness that might well become real beauty when she was a little older. When she smiled, Eden thought she seemed vaguely familiar.

"Eden, this is Kim Rowland. I believe you were in school with her sister, Tina."

"Oh, yes! She was in the class ahead of me," Eden smiled. "How is Tina?"

"All right now, I guess." Kim studied Eden curiously as she answered. "She and Ron were divorced a couple of years ago."

"I'm sorry. I didn't know."

Eden remembered when Tina had eloped with Ron Ainslee. It had been during their last year of high school, and Tina had been two months pregnant at the time but nonetheless enamored of the high romance of her secret marriage.

"Tina gets kind of fed up, being stuck at home with the kids so much," Kim explained. "She has a boy and a girl." She moved to position the cart near Paula.

"Eden will pour today, Kim," Paula instructed her. "My hands are giving me some discomfort," she added apologetically.

58

"You should stop by and see Tina if you get the chance," Kim suggested hopefully as she jockeyed the cart toward Eden. "I'm sure she'd be thrilled if you would."

"I'll do that, although it'll be fall before I'll have the opportunity," Eden agreed. "In the meantime, would you tell her I said hello?"

"Sure thing," the girl replied airily as she left the room.

Eden served Paula her tea, adding sugar and lemon as the older woman requested, and poured a cup for herself. It was delicious; warming and comforting to Eden.

"It's too bad about Tina's divorce," Paula commiserated after they had been silent for a time.

"Yes," Eden replied jauntily to conceal her bitterness. "So many of my old school friends are on their second marriages that I've lost count. There used to be statistics to the effect that married couples had an average of two-point-five children, but the way things are going nowadays, it won't be long before each child has an average of two-point-five mothers and two-point-five fathers."

"It's especially trying for children when their parents separate."

"It's hell," Eden stated emphatically. "I'd never put a child through it." Her vision was suddenly misted by tears, and she bent her head over her teacup.

"I was extremely lucky in my marriage," Paula reminisced. "My husband, Neil, was a marvelous man, a delightful companion and a wonderful father. He was my best friend and my staunchest ally. I was so happy and fulfilled as his wife that my friends were all surprised that I never remarried. After I'd had a few years to recover from the grief and shock of his death, I guess it surprised me too. I suppose he was just too difficult an act for any other man to follow!"

"You're very fortunate," Eden murmured, "but I suspect that to a large extent you created your own luck."

"I'm going to take the chance of trespassing on our friendship by offering you some unsolicited advice, my dear," Paula declared bluntly. "You've always been a nonconformist and, selectively exercised, it can be an admirable trait. Heaven knows you had a lot of justification for being rebellious as a youngster! Just don't fall into the trap of resorting to nonconformity for its own sake—because it's a known quantity and seems safe to you."

Eden choked on her tea, and though her eyes were streaming from a fit of coughing, she registered the older woman's searching gaze. Her blue-gray eyes conveyed her astonishment at the similarity of Paula's advice to a remark Annie had made shortly before her death. Annie had cautioned her more colorfully, saying, "If you flit around and flit around, you're going to land in a cow pie!"

Touched by Paula's concern, she promised, "I'll try not to."

Their conversation turned to lighter topics after that, and the time passed pleasantly until Alex returned to the living room to inform Eden that Beverly Schuyler was waiting to speak to her on the telephone.

"She undoubtedly wants to wish you happiness," he conjectured affably.

Because she knew that Beverly was worried about her, Eden had written to her and filled her in on her plans for the summer. She had told her that Alex and she were going to be married but after several false starts had given up trying to explain satisfactorily by letter that their marriage was to be in name only. She'd finally decided that since the whole situation was so outlandish, it would be easier to let the facts speak for themselves when the annulment was granted in the fall.

She had never imagined that Beverly would discover her whereabouts and call her *here,* at Alex's home. *I should have known,* Eden thought, for she knew from experience that once Beverly Schuyler had resolved to follow a given course, she was as tenacious as a bulldog.

As she went into the library to take the call, Eden wondered fleetingly whether Alex and Beverly had discussed her, but she dismissed the notion as unlikely when Beverly responded to her greeting with characteristic fluting ebullience, obviously unconcerned.

"Eden? Oh, honey, I just can't begin to tell you how delighted Peter and I are for you. You know we wish all the best for you!" Beverly exclaimed. "And your Alex—well, all I can say is, if his voice is any indication, he must be a real hunk!"

In the background at the Schuyler's end of the connection, Eden heard Peter warn playfully, "I heard that, Bev!"

"Pete's here too, Eden," Beverly divulged unnecessarily, "making a nuisance of himself as usual." Though her words were complaining, her tone was indulgent. "He wants to say hello to you too. I'll just put him on so he can speak his piece; then you and I can talk without interruption."

"How the mighty have fallen, eh, Eden?" Peter razzed her without preamble. "You could have knocked me over with a feather when I read your letter and learned that the confirmed spinster was getting married. What brought on the about-face?"

So far she'd been required to say nothing more enlightening than hello, and she felt tongue-tied.

"It was just one of those things," she replied evasively.

"I made some inquiries—strictly out of concern for you—and I've heard nothing but good about your husband."

"You made inquiries?" she echoed, aghast.

"I just asked a couple of people I thought might be acquainted with Alex about him. Nothing formal or out-and-out snoopy," Peter hastened to assure her. "Don't sweat it, okay?"

Don't sweat it, Eden retorted silently. That's easy for you to say!

She supposed she should be grateful that Peter cared enough about her to check up on Alex, but instead she felt like the world's worst impostor.

"Anyway, he sounds like quite a man. He must be to have been able to persuade you to change your mind about marriage!"

"That's *enough,* Peter." Beverly's voice carried over the line.

"Eden"—Beverly must have succeeded in regaining possession of the receiver—"isn't he the most awful tease?" she asked rhetorically. "Men!" she groaned and the single word spoke volumes.

Eden could envision Beverly at this minute. Petite, dark, and good-natured, she was inveterately easygoing unless her personal code of justice was offended, at which point she could become intense and determined. At such times Peter called her Tiger.

Eden remembered one such occasion when they had taken the children to the Fleishhacker Zoo, and a panhandler had unwisely accosted Beverly, asking for a handout. She'd given the young man a sermon on the evils of sloth, argued that he was apparently able-bodied and of at least average intelligence, and should have too much pride to be content to live by the sweat of anyone else's brow. She'd concluded by pointing to Peter junior and Eunice, who were looking on, fascinated by the virago their mother had become.

"Do you have any idea," she'd asked with scathing contempt, "how much it costs just to keep growing children in shoes and peanut butter sandwiches, let alone provide adequately for all the other necessities?"

Regretting his choice of her as an easy touch, the young man had merely nodded.

"Yet you have the audacity to ask *me* for money. No!" she'd announced firmly. "I won't give you a cent. My children need it far more than you!"

The scene had drawn a good-size crowd and, pursued by jeers and catcalls, the panhandler had slunk away in defeat.

Eden was overcome with a longing for the lively yet relaxed pattern of her life in the Schuylers' home that she was unable to shake off after the telephone call had ended. As the afternoon aged into evening the feeling grew and persisted.

Elaine and Jerry had been asked to dinner for a sort of farewell party, and while she appreciated the thoughtfulness that had motivated Paula's invitation to them, her sister and brother-in-law's attitudes toward Eden imposed an additional strain on her. Elaine's manner was aloof, as though she sought to avoid even a semblance of closeness to Eden, and Jerry remained overtly disapproving.

After the meal was over, Eden drifted outdoors, tired of being treated like a pariah by the Reeces. She sauntered along the brick path that wound through the well-tended beds of dahlias and roses that were the showpieces of Paula Lassiter's garden and down the dewy sweep of lawn that sloped toward the arbor.

As she walked toward it through the clinging mist of the fog, the arbor looked ghostly. The grapevines that all but encircled it and trailed their twining branches over the latticed roof were very old, and their shaggy trunks were thick and twisted with years, causing them to resemble a congregation of ancient graybeards.

She rubbed a grape leaf between her fingers and the pungent odor that came forth reminded her of long-ago summer days of childish derring-do. She snapped off one of the tender shoots and bit into it, but the sharp tartness left an aftertaste that brought her back to the present, for it was an appropriate duplication of her feelings about the events of the day. Her wedding day.

When she was a little girl she had often sneaked over here, crawled into the tunnel of leaves between the slatted sides of the arbor and the trunks of the vines, and in the green bower of that hidey-hole, she had found escape from her aunt and uncle's nagging. She had found peace and solace. It had been only coincidence that during the summer when she was twelve years old, she had often seen Alex—and whoever happened to be his girl of the moment—as they kissed and petted in their trysting place inside the arbor. But, she admitted to herself with a transient smile, Alex's amorous activities had introduced a certain spicy element to those occasions.

Driven by an irresistible impulse, Eden parted the vine leaves and, kicking off her high-heeled pumps and making herself as small as possible, edged her way inch by inch into her old sanctuary. The rich, moldy humus smell of the fog-dampened soil rose up to greet her so tangibly that she felt as though it wrapped her in a comfortable, well-worn cloak. But it became a straitjacket when she heard Alex and Jerry approaching, and she felt trapped by the smallness of the space.

When they seated themselves on garden chairs in the arbor, she was forced to become an unwilling eavesdropper to their conversation.

". . . nevertheless, I want you to know how much we appreciate your taking on Eden like this," Jerry was saying obsequiously. "If the Foundation decides to build a research center here, it will be like a breath of fresh air to the local economy. We've needed new industry for as long as I can remember, and the types of development this would foster would be year-round, not seasonal like the timber and fishing operations."

There was the flare of a match, and the aroma of pipe smoke reached Eden before Alex replied dryly, "I realize that, of course, but there wasn't much choice if the project was to proceed as scheduled. I'm doing this basically for personal reasons that are purely selfish as well, so don't try and polish my halo any more than I deserve."

"Frank and Justine are terribly grateful to you." Jerry spoke again, ignoring Alex's disclaimer. "They're relieved to be rid of the embarrassment of Eden's presence for a time. She's been a trial to them for much too long."

"Have they even seen her since she's been back in town," Alex asked without inflection.

"Well . . . no, naturally not." Jerry began by sounding uncertain but ended by being huffy. "Quite the opposite, in fact. They've taken care to avoid seeing her. You couldn't realistically expect them to do otherwise after all the grief she put them through when she was a teen-ager."

He paused expectantly, as though waiting for Alex's agreement, and when this was not forthcoming, he concluded, weakly conciliatory, "I just wanted you to know that we're indebted to you for this." When Alex still made no comment, he said reluctantly, "Well—uh—I know you want to have an early night, so Elaine and I will be on our way."

Eden was simmering with anger as she listened to the shuffling of feet that indicated the two men had risen and left the arbor. While Jerry's opinions were no surprise to her, she felt Alex had betrayed her by offering no defense on her behalf. She had no good reason to expect him to object to Jerry's unflattering summation of her character, yet she couldn't help feeling that he'd let her down by remaining silent. She was married to him—even if it was only a matter of convenience—so didn't he owe her some loyalty?

The white-hot strength of her fury caused the numerous small doubts that had plagued her throughout the day to crystallize into the single chilling conviction that she should never under any circumstances have agreed to become Alex's wife.

## Chapter Five

The brassy sun beat down mercilessly from the un-
clouded blue of the sky as Eden struggled after Alex
up the steep, dusty trail. After catching a predawn
flight from Eureka to Redding and a two-hour drive
from that city to the northeastern boundary of the
wilderness area, they had been hiking since midmorning, and from the position of the sun Eden
judged it was now four or five o'clock. Their hike had
begun with a short, precipitous climb, and then
they'd followed a comparatively easy route along a
ridge for quite a distance. But for the last two hours
they'd been climbing again steadily, and she was
ready to drop with fatigue. She was gasping for
breath, her legs were rubbery and shaking with
weariness, and the straps of her backpack were
chafing her shoulders so that they felt raw.

She wiped the dampness away from her forehead with the back of her hand, leaving a streak of reddish dust that emphasized the pallor of her face, and raised her head fractionally to scan the trail above for Alex.

He was still swinging effortlessly uphill with his long, easy stride. His broad shoulders were unbowed, while she had walked the last mile bent almost double. He'd stripped until, with the exception of his boots, he wore only cutoff jeans that were frayed around the edges, and his sunbronzed legs were powerful, consuming great distances with each step he took—and he looked *cool*!

Dammit, she thought, will he never stop for a breather? It had been ages since the last rest, and she was ready to melt. Her feet were leaden in her cumbersome waffle-stomper boots, and her mouth felt as if it were lined with cotton wool. She considered stopping for a drink from her canteen but decided that if she did, she would never be able to force herself to take another step up the stupid mountain.

Earlier she'd taken the trouble to look about her in admiration at the vast magnificence of the high country. The lower slopes were densely forested with pines and fir, dotted here and there with open spaces of picturesque meadows, their verdancy relieved by the silvery leaves of aspen, the lush purple of lupine, or the blue of one of the many small lakes of the region.

From one jutting eminence on the trail they'd been able to see through a pass in the mountain range to the snow-capped pinnacle of Mount Shasta, and Alex had told her about the unique cult of Californians who believed that a society of humanoids existed in subterranean depths underneath that volcanic cone. Supposedly they were extraterrestrial beings from some planet outside of the solar system. There were those who claimed to have met and spoken with these people.

Further down the trail, on looking up, she had seen above the timberline the craggy, slate-blue marble peaks from which the mountains took their name, and she had felt the stirring of understanding for the message on the signboard that marked the boundary of the wilderness. She couldn't recall exactly what the entire wording had been, but the part about finding "restoration for the soul" that had seemed so exaggerated when she'd read it had begun to have real meaning for her.

Near the beginning of their hike they'd crossed a raging stream, torrential with runoff from the still-melting snows at higher elevations. Think of the stream, she advised herself, and she envisioned it: wet and cold and refreshing. She licked her parched lips and tasted only the saltiness of the perspiration that was rolling off her face.

*How long can I sweat at this rate,* she wondered, *before all that's left of me is a grease spot and a bunch of dry bones on this blast furnace of a trail?* For a moment she tried to calculate the time but gave it up happily when Alex hailed her.

"We've reached the cabin!" he called through the

megaphone of his cupped hands. "I can see it from here."

Eden almost stumbled over her feet in her clumsy rush to reach the spot where he waited on the trail— a kind of minicrest on the unending climb.

When she caught up to him, she was aware, for only an instant, of his concerned observation of her. Then she spotted the cabin. It was not very far and it was downhill. She was revived by the sight of the steep pitch of the cabin roof, just visible through the screen of the pines. Close by it she glimpsed the breeze-rippled surface of a small alpine lake.

In a sudden spate of energy she started to move forward once again, but Alex forestalled her with one hand on her shoulder.

"I'll take your pack the rest of the way," he offered. "You've done very well today but frankly, you look beat!"

"I can manage," she retorted, but he had already unbuckled the belt about her hips that secured the pack and was slipping it from her shoulders. Freed of its weight, she stood erect, gratefully stretching her tortured spine.

"Thank you." Her voice was tinged with resentment of his cavalier treatment, but he ignored it and, with a dismissive wave of his hand, started down the trail.

As they drew nearer, Eden saw that the cabin was an A-frame built of logs that had weathered to a pale silvery color. The side facing the lake was mostly glass, and a good-size porch was built at that end for additional outdoor living-space. It was situated in a small clearing above the lakeshore and sheltered on the three sides away from the water by trees that were tall and sentinel-straight.

Alex had disappeared inside by the time she had climbed the steps to the porch. After stopping for an appreciative look at the view of the lake with its backdrop of forest and, brooding over it all, the sheer rocky cliff that ended high above at the very rim of the mountain, she followed after him.

Inside the cabin it was dim and slightly musty from disuse but wonderfully cooled by the breeze that blew across the lake and through the open front door. Eden collapsed onto the sofa, numb with exhaustion. She heard the sounds of Alex moving around emanating from the loft above her. Inspecting his domain, she thought wryly. Then she fell asleep.

Alex woke her in the early evening, shaking her and calling her incessantly.

"Go 'way," she mumbled, covering her ears with her hands and burrowing with her head beneath the sound barrier of the sofa pillows.

"Wake up, Red. You'll rest more comfortably after you've cleaned up and had some food."

The enticing fragrance of coffee tempted her to open her eyes enough to peek at him through the tangled web of her lashes. She was terribly thirsty.

"Could I have some water?" she croaked.

"Sit up first so I can be sure you're really awake. God," he exclaimed, "you're impossible to rouse!"

She complied cautiously, her overworked muscles complaining. She learned she was one massive ache. She bit her lip to keep from groaning at the pain of the smallest movement.

Alex regarded her knowingly.

"I'll get you a glass of water," he said and left her momentarily.

The water he brought her was deliciously cold and soothing to her dry throat, and the coffee made her feel a little more alert. She sipped it slowly, savoring the rich flavor.

"Thank you. That was very good," she said, complimenting him when her cup was empty. "I feel almost human now."

"I'll show you to the facilities, and you can have a shower. That should complete the transformation."

She followed awkwardly, easing herself forward as he led her down a short hallway and through the small kitchen to the side door of the cabin.

"There's your shower." He indicated the small cubicle that housed the bathroom. "You'll be relieved to hear there's hot water. It's heated with propane. The kitchen stove also uses bottled gas," he explained. "The water is piped by gravity flow from a spring higher up. Tomorrow or the next day I'll show you where the water supply originates and how to check the pipeline."

"Thank you," she repeated, turning blindly toward the bath.

"Don't you want a change of clothes?" he reminded her.

She was close to tears with the pain of moving, and he must have seen this, for he volunteered briskly, "Tell me what you'd like and I'll get it."

She was embarrassed by the idea of his going through her things, but the thought of walking any farther than was absolutely necessary overrode her dismay.

"Oh . . . anything." She stared at the floor, too weak to confront the battery of his eyes.

"Go ahead and hop in the shower. I'll leave your clothes just outside the door." He gave her a gentle shove to get her going. "We'll have to conserve the bottled gas and indulge ourselves with hot showers only occasionally, but use all the hot water you want tonight. I've already showered," he added unnecessarily. She'd known before he told her that he had; he looked so spruce and energetic.

"*Hop in,*" he'd said. That was a laugh! It seemed to take forever to untie her boots and pull them off, to strip off the grubby jeans and long-sleeved shirt he'd insisted she wear, saying with derogatory intonation, "With your skin, you'd be burned to a crisp inside half an hour." She sniffed disdainfully as she recalled this critical remark. She'd always thought her skin was one of her better features and she'd certainly never had any complaints about it before.

She peeled off her bra and panties as well as the heavy socks she'd worn with the boots and stepped under the hot, needle-sharp spray of the shower. It was bliss. She stood without moving for long minutes, allowing the heat of the water to work its miracle and loosen her stiffening muscles before she found some soap in the soap tray—evidently Alex's. It was mildly lime-scented and pleasant. She used it freely, working the lather into her grimy skin and even washing her hair with it before the water started to cool.

On stepping out, she saw there was only one towel on the rack—his. She shrugged and used it without compunction. She caught a drift of the clean lime fragrance that had remained on Alex's towel as she dried herself. Alex smelled like that. It's appropriate that we smell alike: he's my husband, she thought, and even as this occurred to her, she froze.

From the mirror over the sink her image, rosy from the shower, mocked her. She turned away, quickly wrapping the towel around herself, concealing her delicately sloping shoulders and proud, pink-tipped breasts, the narrow rib cage and small waist that flared to the soft, rounded fullness of her hips.

She dressed quickly in the clothing Alex had deposited outside for her. He'd left only bikini panties, shorts, a bandeau top, and some thonged sandals. For someone who didn't appreciate her skin, it seemed he intended she should show quite a bit of it.

She combed her hair with her pocket comb, tidied the bath, put her soiled things in the hamper, and carried her boots with her when she returned timorously to the kitchen.

75

Alex glanced up at her as she came in, rapidly summing up her appearance.

"You look better," he said matter-of-factly. "Let's eat."

She felt strangely deflated and attempted to overcome it by asking herself silently, What did you expect—that he'd suddenly leap on you, driven mad with uncontrollable passion? She smiled at the ridiculousness of the idea. Alex was the least driven, most controlled man she'd ever met.

"What are you grinning about?"

"It was a private joke," she replied cryptically.

He looked at her somewhat sourly as he handed her a plate. They ate in silence. The omelet he had prepared from freeze-dried eggs was unexpectedly delicious, but Eden was too tired to eat very much and excused her lack of appetite by saying as much when he commented on it. He refilled her coffee cup, and she was able to enjoy that.

"Come along," he said abruptly, startling her. She'd been nearly asleep again. "I have some liniment that will be good for what ails you."

"I'm not nearly so sore now. It isn't necessary," she protested.

"Wait till tomorrow," he predicted, not unsympathetically. "You'll know the meaning of real suffering then."

He ushered her into the main room, where he positioned her facedown on the couch, while he sat on the edge at the level of her thighs as he massaged her back and shoulders, working the liniment in

76

deeply, impersonally shifting the narrow elasticized top she wore in order to cover her back completely from her hips upward. That explains his choice of clothes for me, she thought.

"Ugh! It smells awful," she complained.

She wrinkled her nose with distaste but other than that she felt too contented to move.

Alex thrust the bottle at her and delivered an enlivening swat to her bottom.

"You'd better put some on your legs," he ordered, and she swung her feet to the floor and began smoothing miserly amounts of it onto her thighs. She sensed he was watching her closely and concentrated on spreading the medicine evenly over her legs until she realized he was busily occupied with lighting the fire he'd already laid in the fireplace.

She looked at him surreptitiously, unwillingly admiring the deft economy of his movements as, satisfied with the fire, he proceeded to light the kerosene lamps so that the dusky light in the cabin was warmed by their mellow, golden glow.

When he'd finished with the lanterns, Alex extracted his tobacco pouch from his pocket and stood with his booted foot propped on the hearth, leaning with one elbow against the mantel as he filled his pipe. His long, beautifully formed fingers were strong and capable as they tamped the tobacco into the bowl, and Eden stared, fascinated by their dexterity and by the sinewy play of muscles in his forearms revealed by the rolled-back cuffs of his shirtsleeves. He had exchanged his raveled shorts for close-fitting jeans and he'd left his shirt mostly unbuttoned, displaying a disturbing expanse of his chest.

He struck a match against the keystone of the fireplace and lighted his pipe, puffing steadily until the tobacco glowed an even orangey red beneath the surface layer of gray ash.

Eden put the top back on the bottle of liniment and after setting it aside, she slouched deeper into the upholstery of the sofa. She glanced quickly away when Alex suddenly looked at her as though trying to catch her in the act of studying him.

"I find it hard to believe you're Elaine's twin," he said.

"Well, don't let it throw you," Eden replied crisply. "Most people have a similar reaction."

"Why?" he asked tersely.

"I should think it would be obvious. While we bear a certain family resemblance to each other, our personalities are so different. Elaine is conventional. She can be relied on to do what's expected of her, to want all the 'proper' things from life. She has her act together, while I—" She shrugged, pretending a nonchalance she did not feel.

"What I meant was, why do you assume that my comment was intended as a criticism of you? It could have been a simple observation—or even a compliment."

"As I've already said, most people react that way."

"Do I detect a note of self-pity in your voice?" His tone was mocking.

78

"No!" she replied, almost explosive with feeling. "Oh, Lord, I hope not. That's one fault I do try to avoid like the plague."

"That's one thing in your favor then." He smiled at her. "It's a relief to know you'll admit to having at least one virtue."

His smile broadened, and his eyes glinted with humor as his discerning observation of her detected the swift tensing of her body in response to his comment.

"Next time maybe you'll warn me ahead of time when you're keeping score," she retorted stiffly.

"Afraid of spoiling your image?" he drawled.

Eden did not reply but returned his gaze, she hoped stonily. From their reunion at Elaine and Jerry's she had sensed that only danger lay ahead for her if she were to allow him to penetrate her defenses, but only now was she beginning to realize the shape it might assume and how very threatening he was to her.

"What did Jerry mean when he said people were just beginning to give you the benefit of the doubt again?" The incisiveness of the question was disguised by the softness of his voice as he asked it.

"Don't tell me he didn't fill you in with all the details about my lurid past."

"He told me one side of it." He drew thoughtfully on his pipe, his palm curving around the bowl. The cloud of smoke that wreathed his face as he exhaled prevented her from seeing his expression clearly as he invited, "Now I'd like to hear your version."

"Are you serious?" Her voice was high-pitched, almost shrill with disbelief.

"Never more serious, Red," Alex assured her with patent sincerity, and she was astonished to feel a hot rush of tears at the backs of her eyes. She looked down at her hands, which were resting on her thighs. They were curled into fists and were too revealing of her emotions. She consciously tried to relax, breathing deeply and slowly and closing her eyelids in an effort to stem her rising agitation.

Alex crossed to the couch and sat down beside her, stretching his long legs comfortably before him.

"We're going to be living in each others pockets for the next few months and we'll have to feel we can rely on each other—possibly for our very survival and in all likelihood, for the preservation of our sanity. It would make things much easier all around if we play it straight."

Her sweetly molded chin was tilted at a stubborn angle as she listened to him, wary of his interest in her.

"Granted," she said, "but what makes you so certain that my version is any different than Jerry's?"

"Let's just say that there seem to be certain glaring contradictions between what I've heard about you and the way you behave."

"Whatever I might tell you, it's not likely to change your opinion of me," Eden countered. "You'll believe whatever it is you want to believe about me anyway."

"That's nothing more than rationalization," he

pointed out evenly. "You're trying to convince your-self that you don't care what people think of you—what *I* think of you—and if you'll be honest with yourself, you'll admit you *do* care."

Eden sprang lightly to her feet and, though she felt like running, she forced herself to walk slowly to the window. The sun had set in a blaze of crimson, pink, and gold behind the jagged crest of the mountain, and the brilliance of the sky was reflected by the smooth, dark surface of the lake. She stared fixedly at the scene, arrested by the violent beauty of it.

Alex was right about one thing, she acknowl-edged. She did care about his opinion of her. She leaned her forehead against the coolness of the win-dow and felt her defiance draining from her, leaving her peculiarly defenseless and aware of her own vul-nerability where he was concerned, yet, at the same time, exhilarated.

No one but Annie had ever asked to hear her side of the story before. She was stunned to hear herself saying as much aloud and darted a look at him over her shoulder, daring him to challenge the honesty of her statement.

"Then this is a chance you can't afford to pass up, isn't it?" He was smiling again, but this time in en-couragement.

She turned back to the window. It was dark enough outside now that she could observe him in the mirrorlike glass.

"I suppose Jerry told you my uncle invited me to

leave his home when I was barely seventeen." Her voice was steady. "Did he tell you why?"

"He said it had something to do with drugs."

"Yes. Uncle Frank found a cache of pills—uppers, downers, you name it—in my bureau. Also cocaine, LSD, marijuana—a veritable pharmacy was in that drawer!"

"They weren't yours though," Alex reasoned calmly. "You're far too independent to ever allow yourself to habitually use even nonaddictive drugs, let alone get hooked on narcotics."

"No," she sighed. It was a relief to say it aloud after all this time. "They weren't mine."

"They were Elaine's," Alex said. It was a statement.

"If you know so much, why ask me?" Her voice was sharp with irritation.

He ignored her petulance and asked, "Why did you take the blame? Was it just that you were accustomed to protecting Elaine?"

"I—no! I don't know. It just didn't seem right to . . . to—"

"To squeal on her?" he prompted.

"Yes."

"Aah!" He breathed the exclamation softly. "It was a matter of principle then."

He smiled sardonically. He was goading her, trying to get her to react strongly, and he was not disappointed. She turned on him, white-lipped with anger.

"Yes," she shouted. "Yes, dammit! Make fun of it if you like, but it *is* a matter of principle."

"I agree," Alex said smoothly.

She watched him wordlessly as she fought to regain her composure. Her head felt as though it were whirling with the seething of her muddled thoughts.

"You confuse me," she admitted, shaking her head as she slumped weakly against the window.

"I don't mean to do that." He knocked the dottle out of his pipe, making a project out of cleaning it thoroughly with his penknife. "I wanted to make you lose your temper, that's all." He watched her intently as he explained, "With a few notable exceptions, you do such a fine impression of someone who is totally uninvolved, totally uncommitted, who doesn't give a damn for anything, I needed convincing it wasn't true. So now we both know how deeply you do care, and you can take that chip off your shoulder, drop the act, and be yourself."

"Look who's talking," she accused. "Mr. Cool himself."

"Touché," he responded easily, grinning. "But now that the preliminaries are over, can we get down to the main bout?"

"Will you give me a return match tomorrow night," she bargained, "with me asking you the questions?"

"That seems fair enough," he agreed mildly.

Eden moved to the chair opposite the couch and sat down, squarely confronting him.

"All right then, Mr. Interlocutor, what do you want to know?"

"The truth, of course!" Alex raised one eyebrow, and his lean cheeks creased with his lopsided smile. "Just start at the beginning."

Eden leaned back in the chair and let her glance fall away from his before she spoke.

"Elaine had been experimenting with drugs for some time. She'd gotten in with a bad crowd at school, and I could tell from changes in her behavior she was on something. It got so that most of the time she was either really high or semiconscious. But the drugs my uncle found weren't hers alone."

"Why do you say that?"

"Elaine told me. Besides, where would she have gotten the money for that amount of narcotics?"

"I can think of at least two ways," Alex rejoined dryly. "Dealing or—" He stopped when he saw Eden's stricken expression.

"Look, Elaine may not have the strongest character, but I don't believe she's capable of that. Anyway, as I said before, she's conventional. She's capable of minor infractions, but never that! She told me that she had hidden the drugs for some of her friends, and I believed her."

She glared at Alex, as though expecting him to disagree, before continuing. "Another reason I didn't tell Uncle Frank the truth was that I didn't think Elaine could make it on her own. She was so gullible and—well, naive, I guess."

"Didn't it ever occur to you that you were the one who was gullible and naive to shield Elaine?"

"No," she replied firmly, "because I knew exactly what I was doing."

"Did you?" His expression was dubious but he did not belabor the issue. "What happened then?"

"I spent that night with Annie Holmes, and the next day I took the bus to Santa Rosa. I had some money saved, and Annie loaned me a little. It wasn't much of a nest egg, but I found a job almost immediately, so it was enough. I worked as a waitress for about two years and managed to complete the requirements for my high school diploma. Then I took the job with the Schuylers in San Francisco so I could pick up some college credits. After I was injured, I was unable to work and I had no money so—" She had spoken so rapidly that the words had fairly tumbled out but now her voice trailed into silence.

"You're glossing things over a bit," Alex commented. "Beverly Schuyler told me the facts about your accident when I spoke with her on the phone yesterday. From what she told me I can guess the rest—you were forced to return home to recuperate and decided to take the opportunity to try to repair the damage to your reputation."

She nodded. "I'd kept in touch with Annie, so I knew she'd stopped taking in lodgers a few years ago, and she was lonely. She offered to help me till I was able to work again. I thought Elaine and Jerry might also."

"And did they?" He watched impassively as the color drained from her face.

"They—Jerry offered me a sum of money if I'd leave Eureka and sign an agreement not to return," she admitted reluctantly.

"Why do you think they believed you were so mercenary that you'd accept such an offer?"

"I—I'd told Elaine some—" Her voice faltered. She couldn't bring herself to say the word.

"Lies," he supplied tersely.

"Yes," she agreed faintly.

"About the commune where you were supposed to have lived."

"Yes."

"About the number of men you claimed you'd been with."

"Yes." Her response was nearly unintelligible. She kept her face averted so that her acute embarrassment would be less evident.

Alex stood abruptly, towering over her so that she had the urge to cower back into the chair and had to steel herself not to. Her fingers nervously traced the colorful weave of the Navaho blanket draped over the back of the chair.

"Why?" He spoke softly. "Why did you tell such lies about yourself?"

Eden shook her head helplessly. "It was stupid of me, I know." She looked up at him and her eyes showed her torment. "It was just that Elaine wasn't satisfied with the truth when I told it to her. She kept asking questions about how I'd gotten by all that time, and from the way she phrased them, it was obvious what she expected—wanted—to hear. Her fantasies got wilder and wilder, and she was just so—avid, so eager. It was as though it gave her some kind of cheap, vicarious thrill to think the worst of me. I—it sickened me."

"So you pandered to her prurient interest by agreeing with her suggestions," he stated brusquely.

She covered her eyes with one shaking hand and remained silent.

"You little fool." Although he hadn't raised his voice above a whisper, it was fierce with anger. "Didn't it occur to you that Elaine would derive a perverted pleasure from passing such juicy stories along over her bridge games and teacups?"

"No. I never thought—" she began unsteadily and Alex interrupted.

"At last we've arrived at the truth. *You never thought!* You just blindly reacted. I hope you've learned a lesson, and that that particular failing won't be in evidence this summer."

He turned and strode to the fireplace and with quick, disjointed motions that demonstrated how nearly depleted his patience with her was, he began banking the fire.

"You can have the downstairs bedroom." He kept his back to her. His shoulders were rigid with condemnation. "It's at the end of the hall. You can take one of the lanterns with you. And you'd better turn in *now,*" he ordered curtly. "It's been one hell of a long day."

## Chapter Six

The blank page of the diary accused her—of what? Of idiocy? Of cowardice? Eden chewed absently on the end of her pen as she pondered this. Was what she felt merely a natural aversion to sharing her most private thoughts and feelings with complete strangers? With the scientists at the Foundation who would review her personal record of the summer? With the data-entry clerks and programmers who would computerize it? Was it concern for their reactions to her jottings that created her reluctance? Was she afraid they would deem her a fool? Laugh at her? Pity her?

Perhaps it was because she didn't want to confront herself. While she disliked confessing it to the diary, she freely acknowledged to herself that she was bored. It was *why* she should be that eluded her.

She'd never had any problem with occupying her mind or otherwise entertaining herself before. In fact, she'd always thought she was rather resourceful, and the psychometrist who had administered the series of tests she'd been required to take prior to becoming a subject in the study had confirmed this. He'd made no other specific comments as to the results, but he hadn't thrown up his hands in discouragement either.

So why this terrible ennui? This was only her first full day here, and it was obvious she could not hope to survive the summer unless she pinpointed the cause and did something to correct it.

The day had begun well enough. The mixture of humiliation and resentment she'd felt at Alex's treatment of her the night before had receded with the darkness, and when the sun had wakened her this morning, she'd felt confident and in command of herself once again. She was determined there would be no further lapses like the one of the night before that might result in the development of unwanted intimacies between Alex and herself.

She dressed and prepared for the day slowly, discovering that Alex's warning had been justified, for she did indeed learn the meaning of real suffering as every muscle protested yesterday's abuse of it and clamored for relief. Once dressed, she unpacked her belongings and put them away.

Her room was pine-paneled, as was the rest of the cabin, small, and furnished simply with bunk beds, a bureau, and a nightstand. There was a wall shelf for the paperback books she'd had brought in by the packer, and it provided enough space for her chess set as well. She'd also brought some needlepoint tapestries to work on to help to pass the time. Her things tidily stored, she made her bed and left the room.

Though it was only eight o'clock, the main room and kitchen were neat and deserted. There was a note from Alex propped on the counter near the stove, and she assessed his firmly erect, precise handwriting as she read the succinct message.

> Coffee's in the pot. Take it easy today. See you at lunch.

As she drank her coffee and orange juice and ate some oatmeal, she heard the muffled sounds of typing coming from the sleeping loft and wondered what he was working on that would take the rest of the morning.

It required only a few minutes effort to restore the kitchen to the orderly state in which she'd found it, and she suddenly realized how difficult it might be to fill the time.

As the morning progressed, so did her restlessness, punctuated by the slow sounds of the typewriter. Alex might be many things, but he certainly was not an expert typist. It seemed he was more of the hunt-and-peck caliber. She wandered from room to room, unable to settle to any of the diversions she'd brought with her.

During lunch Alex was preoccupied and uncommunicative. He excused himself and returned to the loft as soon as the meal was over, leaving her to clear things away. Again this was quickly accomplished, and the afternoon stretched interminably ahead of Eden.

For a while she sat on the deck, and the beneficent warmth of the sun was a balm to her aching muscles. Soon she felt limber enough to attempt a stroll to the lakeshore but the steep, downhill portion of the path nearest the cabin was too taxing for her to negotiate, and she was regretfully forced to postpone any exploring until the next day.

She returned to her frustrated pacing. Even that was difficult, limping as she was. Again and again her eyes sought the ladder to the loft but, curious as she was to know what Alex was working on, as filled with longing as she was for the companionship of another person, she would not permit herself the indulgence of climbing to the loft.

"I wouldn't give him the satisfaction," she muttered to herself.

A thorough inventory of the cabinets in the kitchen and the pantry just off it occupied her for a time. Most of their foodstuffs were either dried or freeze-dried, although there were a few canned goods. There were ample cleaning supplies.

She drew up a meal plan for the next few days and decided she would try her hand at baking some bread the next morning.

When she found she was continually consulting

91

her wristwatch, it occurred to her that this was the one article she'd be better off without. It only underscored how slowly the day was passing. She removed it, and after decisively tucking it away in a dresser drawer in her room, she resumed her restive prowling.

Since she wore no watch, she had no idea what time it was when Alex finally descended from the loft, but she estimated it to be about five o'clock. He rummaged through the tool shed near the cabin and dug out a rod and reel, assembling them while Eden looked on enviously.

"With any kind of luck, we'll have trout for dinner," he announced as, whistling a popular tune deplorably off-key, he loped down the path to the lake.

Eden felt like screaming after him and throwing things. Instead she'd decided to write her entry for the day in her diary and was now confronted by the empty page. She riffled the pages of the thick notebook, thinking that there were an awful lot of them to fill.

Would she constantly feel she must censor her musings, order her emotions so that she would be unashamed about disclosing them? It didn't seem right to be less than honest, but what exactly was the truth?

Last night Alex had accused her of being impetuous, of not stopping to think her actions through, and he'd called that the truth.

She sighed and resignedly closed the diary. She'd try again later tonight. Probably the only thing wrong with her was that her enforced physical inactivity had led to the unfamiliar mental lassitude that had persisted for this whole wasted day.

As if a kindly fate was smiling on her for having survived the day, the evening turned out to be a pleasant one. Alex grilled the trout on the outdoor fireplace while Eden prepared a package of freeze-dried food mysteriously labeled VEGETABLE STEW and made some sourdough biscuits. They ate on the deck, seated at the redwood picnic table, as the shadows of twilight deepened into dusk.

The trout had a subtly smoked flavor and were firm-fleshed, tender, and succulent; the stew turned out to be delicious; the biscuits so light, they melted in one's mouth. After Eden cleared their dishes away, she rejoined Alex, who had remained outside. As they drank their coffee he smoked his pipe, and they watched the night sky until the stars pierced its velvety darkness with diamond-bright clusters.

It was so quiet, the smallest sounds were magnified by comparison—the occasional sighing of the breeze through the pines, the soft flutter of moths at the lighted window of the cabin, the sibilant whisper of some small nocturnal animal scuffling about in the tall grass.

Whether it was the tranquillity of the scene, the excellence of the meal, Alex's easy company, or the fact that she felt better physically after having had another hot shower, Eden was optimistically expectant.

Reluctantly breaking the silence, she asked quietly, "Who was it that suggested me for the study?"

"My mother was the first one who mentioned you as a possibility," Alex replied, "and when Milt and I had checked you out, we decided to approach you about it."

"Checked me out," she echoed doubtfully.

"Only as to your matching the qualifications that were needed," he reassured her.

It became evident he was not going to reveal what the traits were that they had been looking for when he added nothing further to his explanation. Disappointed by the incompleteness of his response, Eden succumbed to her curiosity and inquired, "Why did you agree to participate in the study?"

"As a favor to Milt, and because it gives me the distraction-free environment I need to work on something I've been interested in for a long time."

"Is that what you've been doing today?"

"Yes—organizing some of my notes." He was quiet for a time, sprawled comfortably in his chair. "I work in one of the Van Damme Foundation's divisions—a think tank in Santa Barbara."

"I suppose you're actually Doctor Lassiter," she said. "You're a microbiologist, aren't you?"

"Yes, although my field is really a more specialized one within that broader sphere. For want of a more descriptive title, I'd call it genetic engineering."

"But what exactly do you do?"

"I've been researching ways and means of creating new bacteria that will perform useful services for mankind." He chuckled and qualified his statement further. "In lay terms, breeding the little devils."

"It's unreal," Eden laughed dazedly. "I once met a coffee-bean breeder from Brazil, and now I've met a bacteria breeder from Santa Barbara." It sounded awesome and futuristic. "But what kinds of things can bacteria do?"

"You may have heard of a recently developed strain that breaks down petroleum and has the potential use of cleaning up oil spills. As part of their metabolic processes others manufacture enzymes or antiviral substances such as interferon. It's an entirely new and exciting frontier of science, and a highly promising one."

He quirked an eyebrow at her as he went on. "It also promises to be very lucrative now that the way is clear for private corporations to patent the strains for which they've underwritten research costs. Profits could run to billions, because the courts have decided that a living organism can be patented—although, as one Supreme Court justice pointed out, the bacteria might get around such a ruling by reproducing themselves."

"And this kind of research is what you're working on here?" she persisted.

"No," he answered tersely.

"If it's top secret or something—" she began and Alex interrupted sharply.

"No, it's not restricted information or anything like that." He stirred in his chair, and Eden sensed he was reticent about revealing exactly what it was

95

his project involved. "Actually I'm working on a book—a novel."

"A novel!" she exclaimed, obviously taken aback by his disclosure. "What kind of novel?"

"It's science fiction-fantasy."

He sounded relieved. Had he expected her to be amused by this revelation?

"A novel," she repeated, accustoming herself to the idea. "How long have you been working on it?"

"The writing itself, six months or so, though it's been kicking around in the back of my mind for longer than that. I hope to finish the final draft this summer. I've reached the point where I've begun editing and polishing it."

"I heard you typing most of the day."

"Yes," he admitted dryly. "At the rate I'm going, it will take a year just to type it."

"Could I help?" Eden asked shyly, afraid he would rebuff her offer. "I could do some of the typing for you."

"I thought you'd never ask!"

His teeth flashed whitely as he smiled, and Eden found herself smiling back at him without reserve. Unexpectedly Alex's expression sobered and became guarded.

"I'd be very grateful if you would," he said.

"I'd be happy to," she responded honestly and found herself confessing, "I was about ready to climb the walls today with boredom." Alex looked at her, suddenly concerned, and she quipped, "The only thing that stopped me was that my legs were too darned sore!"

"We'll have to work out some kind of schedule for chores and recreation to minimize that problem." His voice was deep and thoughtful. "It's one of the major hazards we'll have to face this summer. You should have said something sooner—but then, you're not a complainer, are you?"

He remembered the fortitude she'd shown on the trail the day before, her dogged refusal to relinquish her pack.

"I think today was a hard one for me because I was forced to remain so inactive," Eden theorized. "But what did the pioneer settlers do?"

"Climbed the walls," he answered evenly. "A lot of them, especially the women, didn't survive the isolation of the frontier. You've heard of cabin fever?" At her nod he continued. "It's not a normal situation, being as secluded as we are. People require the company of other people for their well-being."

Through the gloomy light he could see the pale oval of her small face. Her usually smooth brow was drawn with worry.

"So how do we minimize the effects of our seclusion?"

"By keeping busy," he replied calmly, "physically and mentally. By being imaginative and creative with our leisure time and most of all," he emphasized, "by doing as you've done tonight—sharing whatever rough spots we have with each other."

In the weeks that followed they developed a routine that went well for them. Early mornings were devoted to various chores. Their roles were quite traditional in that Alex did the outdoor jobs and heavy maintenance while Eden was, for the most part, responsible for the housewifely tasks. She offered to prepare most of their meals so that Alex would have more free time to get on with his book. Besides, she enjoyed cooking.

From midmorning to midafternoon Eden worked at the typewriter on the final draft of the manuscript. She was impressed with the quality of Alex's prose and fascinated by the story as it unfolded to her.

In the book Alex dealt with a classical confrontation between good and evil, as self-perpetuating machines sought to take over the earth. Though they were mythical creatures, the personae were so deftly drawn and vividly lifelike that they seemed human.

It became even more apparent to her than before that Alex was an astute observer of people and far from ignorant about women. At times she was astounded by the depth of his insight into the character of his heroine. It was unlikely he'd had any personal experience with the feeling of frustration that resulted from being slotted into certain roles or denied opportunity because of his gender, so how did he manage to describe it so realistically?

When Eden had completed her typing for the day, Alex and she went their separate ways for a time. She would write in her diary, do her personal laundry, read, or explore the trails in the vicinity of the cabin.

Alex had told her that it had been built by a lumber company as living quarters for one of their foresters in the early 1950s when there had been a logging operation several miles away. The materials for the construction of the cabin and its furniture had been delivered over the logging road, long since abandoned and reclaimed by the forest. On one of her hikes Eden had found traces of the old road.

As she gained more confidence in her skills with the use of a map and compass, she expanded the range of her explorations. In the course of her wanderings she often encountered mule deer and occasionally she surprised a slow-moving porcupine or startled a grouse into flight.

On some evenings Alex and she would wait in a blind of pine bows near the game trail by the lake and watch the deer when they came for their evening drink. The bears were plentiful and in the early morning they ritually watched for one in particular that gamboled comically on the beachfront near the cabin, playing with her two cubs.

Eden came to relish the feeling of being at one with nature that she found in the pristine forests of the mountains and she discovered that she also had a clearer understanding as to why some of the American Indian tribes had worshiped certain natural manifestations—different animals, the sun, the moon, the wind, or rain.

She knew that at least one of the tribes in the northern California area had paid homage to the redwood tree, that awe-inspiring most ancient living thing. There was an undeniable logic in venerating the redwoods, in elevating them to the status of gods, for they were towering giants that seemed to touch the very sky; they appeared to be as immortal as their botanical name, *Sequoia sempervirens*—literally translated, "ever-living"—implied.

They were virtually indestructible, having inherent protection against most insect pests, parasites, and diseases. Even fire often did no more than scourge them, protected as they were by their armor of thick bark. They withstood the most degrading mutilations; you could blast a tunnel in them for cars to drive through or hollow them out and build a gift shop inside to attract the tourists, and they survived even that desecration.

It had taken modern man to bring about their demise, to end a life begun thousands of years before with callous indifference, to kill them with the assistance of axes and chainsaws and then blithely to call that progress.

Considering all this, Eden decided that the early Indians had been closer to the truth in their primitive religious practices than some of the so-called civilized people of today who worshiped only material things.

As June waned and July began Alex pronounced that the water in the lake was warm enough for swimming. It was still too cold to stay in for more than a few minutes at a time, but it was a refreshing pastime in the heat of the day and a welcome change of pace. Neither of them swam alone, because the frigid temperatures of the water increased the danger of cramp to a lone swimmer.

In the evenings they spent some time together. Mostly they just talked, although one night Alex produced a guitar and they sang folk songs and country-and-western tunes. After having heard him whistle so tonelessly, Eden was delighted to find that he had a deep, true baritone voice. She would have preferred simply to listen to him, but he'd insisted she join in, and finally she had, with more enthusiasm than talent.

Occasionally they played chess or gin, but this was done in a desultory way, without real competition, since they concentrated more on conversation than on the game. Alex tried to teach her to play draw poker, but he gave it up as a lost cause when she persisted in trying to fill inside straights.

Sometimes they both read, companionably quiet, or Alex read and she worked on her needlepoint.

The Foundation had provided a few "surprises" for them, and they resorted to these on weekends. Among them was origami paper, which they folded to make paper airplanes. They had a contest to see whose plane could fly the farthest, which Alex won. Eden's original design refused to travel in a straight line, no matter what alterations she made to it. However, it did the most aerobatics.

"What amazes me," Alex said, "is that yours flies at all. From the looks of it, I'd have thought that, like the bumble bee, flight was an aerodynamic impossibility for it!"

There were dominoes, and when they tired of playing the usual game with them, they made intricate chains for the fun of watching them topple.

Eden's favorite diversion though, was the roller skates. When Alex found them, she gasped with delight. "I love it! I haven't skated for years."

She eagerly rolled up the braided scatter rugs, and as she laced the boots, laughing and only half jesting, she said, "I've always dreamed of working in one of those huge libraries or offices where the messengers wear skates."

"You're certainly easy to please," Alex commented, grinning indulgently as they linked hands and skated around the room, weaving about the furniture.

They skated remarkably well together and after some practice they were able to perform more complicated dance steps.

"It's too bad we don't have a radio or record player," Eden said, sighing regretfully as they waltzed.

Her cheeks were delicately flushed and her eyes were sparkling with pleasure. When she looked up at Alex, he smiled down at her and his hand at her waist pulled her marginally closer to him. He sobered and suddenly stopped skating. His eyes darkened as they lingered on her mouth and for an instant she thought he intended to kiss her, but she was wrong, for he released her and said brusquely, "That's enough for now."

Her pulses were racing with the awareness of him and she knew it was for the best that he'd stopped when he had. She refused to admit that she was disappointed.

All in all, Eden was surprised at their compatibility, especially since they were such different types. She was impulsive, while Alex was deliberate. Although she'd never worn her heart on her sleeve, she tended toward volatility, while he was cool. Her upbringing had been haphazard, almost bohemian, while his had been orderly. She had a tendency to go off on tangents, while he set a goal for himself, and though he was in no way a plodder, he never lost sight of his objective.

If anything, Alex's dissimilarities to her made him more interesting, and she looked forward to his company with ever-increasing eagerness.

In view of this and with the undemanding, easy give-and-take quality of their relationship well established, Eden could not comprehend why she felt an odd tension as she watched Alex splitting logs for firewood one hot afternoon.

Because it was so warm, he'd removed his shirt and hung it on a nearby tree branch, and his torso was hard and muscular, browned by the sun to a rich teak shade. The smooth skin of his chest was lightly pelted with rough, dark hair and his shoulders were broad and athletic as he swung the ax with a powerful, fluid grace.

She derived sensual pleasure from simply watching him, from admiring the way his long fingers and broad palms gripped the ax handle. No matter what he did, there was a sureness about him, a well-coordinated efficiency of motion that was magnificently self-confident.

She observed him as he bent to position a new log on the chopping block. His hair had grown long enough to follow its natural inclination and it curled crisply, almost wildly, about the sweatband he'd wrapped around his forehead. If anything, it increased his attractiveness. His profile was ruggedly handsome, spare, and uncompromising with its lean cheeks, straight strong-boned nose, and square jaw.

The sound of the ax blade biting into the chopping block rang out, and he straightened, flexing his shoulders and rubbing his hands together.

"How about a swim?" he called and, after nodding agreement, Eden ran to her room and got into her modest two-piece bathing suit.

The blue-and-white stripes of the material enhanced her tan, achieved with extreme caution because her fair skin burned so easily.

The freckles on her nose had darkened also and, much to her discouragement, showed more prominently than before. For a time, Alex had alternated calling her Freckles and Red. Disturbed that he had so accurately zeroed in on the two physical characteristics she least liked about herself by labeling her with these nicknames, she'd asked him one night why he never called her properly by her name.

Feigning a thunderstruck expression that reduced her hard-won dignity to giggles, he'd drawled lazily, "Golly, gee, ma'am! I didn't realize I never used your name." That he'd evaded answering her didn't occur to her until later.

She sighed as she collected her beach towel and suntan lotion and wriggled her bare feet into her sandals. Alex had accused her of not being open, but on certain topics he gave away very little of himself.

One night they'd somehow got into a debate on the subject of marriage, and she'd asked him why he hadn't married.

"How quickly they forget!" He imbued the words with long-suffering tolerance. "I *am* married, Red—to you," he reminded her with a teasing grin.

To her chagrin she blushed.

"You know what I mean," she exclaimed with some exasperation. "Please be serious."

He passed his hand in front of his face as though wiping away his amusement.

"Very well," he replied gravely. "I'll give you a straightforward answer to your question. I haven't married before because I've never met a woman who stimulated me and satisfied me both sexually and intellectually, and I refuse to settle for frustration or boredom for the rest of my life."

His face was inscrutable as he observed her.

"Now, turnabout is fair play, so you tell me *seriously*," he stressed, "why you haven't married."

"Because I stopped believing in fairy tales long ago," she answered lightly. "I looked around and saw that love usually doesn't endure, and that romantic illusions to the contrary are only pipe dreams."

"There speaks the cynic," he intoned harshly. "Why not admit you're too damn afraid to take the chance of being hurt."

It was the closest they'd come to having an argument since their first night at the cabin, and Eden had felt deprived and lonely when he'd turned on his heels with disgust and stalked out of the main room, leaving her on her own for the rest of the evening. She couldn't even work up a self-righteous anger at him because, after all, he was right about her.

In violation of their rules, Alex was already swimming when she arrived at the narrow strip of sandy beach they preferred, paralleling the shoreline with his expert crawl stroke.

Eden dropped her towel and, kicking off her sandals, she plunged into the water, diving into the chill depths of it before her mind could dread its iciness and cause painful hesitation. Difficult as it was to become adjusted to the coldness of the lake, it was worth it. The water was silky and clear, and she left it reluctantly, only when her teeth began to chatter. She emerged from the lake tingling and refreshed.

After giving herself a vigorous rubdown with her towel, she spread it out in a sunny spot and lay prone, her head cradled by her folded arms, as she basked in the sun and let it warm her. She was almost asleep when the hot, prickly feeling on the tender backs of her knees warned her it was time to change position if she wanted to avoid sunburn. She sat up, bending her slender legs and wrapping her arms about her knees.

Alex had come out of the water also and was looking at her, standing motionless on the bank. She could not see his expression, for the sun was behind him, shadowing his face and limning the hard, masculine outline of his tawny body with gold so that he seemed to radiate light and heat.

Eden's breath constricted in her throat. Her chest felt tight. There was something about his stance that struck her as being predatory, as if he were watching and waiting for some signal from her. He started toward her with his long, supple stride, and her pulses raced; she was suddenly light-headed, dizzy.

The next thing Eden was aware of was that Alex was cradling her in his arms, his hands warm on her back, his face pale under his tan as he looked down at her.

"My God, Red. What happened?"

"I—I think I forgot to breathe," she stammered. Her eyelids fluttered down to shut out the sight of the tender gleam in his dark eyes.

"You silly little fool," he muttered affectionately.

His lips brushed hers in a gentle salute, so swift and light she might have imagined it, and though she wanted to creep closer to the strong breadth of his chest, she forced herself to remain inert. She wished he would wrap her more tightly in his arms, hold her with more than fondness. She wished he would crush her close to him, kiss her with passion, and touch her with desire.

Recognition dawned with the shattering force of an explosion behind her closed eyelids. *I love him,* she silently admitted to herself, and knew the bitter taste of her own despair.

## Chapter Seven

"There's Ursa Major." Alex pointed it out, incredibly bright and clear, removed as they were from any kind of artificial lights, and incredibly close from their campsite on the lofty peak of the mountain. They had climbed the mountain earlier that day and had come prepared to spend the night so that Eden might have her first lesson in astronomy from the most advantageously possible spot.

"But that's the Great Bear," she murmured, contrarily using the common name by which she knew it.

"The correct scientific name is Ursa Major," Alex advised her. "Now, do you see Ursa Minor?"

"Do you mean the Little Bear?"

"Ursa Minor," he repeated. His voice was edged

with sternness, as if she'd committed some terrible offense.

"Yes, I see it," she answered, subdued.

"Now, Polaris—"

"The North Star." She interrupted mischievously this time. She could practically hear Alex gnashing his teeth with irritation at her irreverence.

"Polaris," he insisted implacably, "is part of Ursa Minor. It's the last star in the handle of the dipper."

"Don't you mean Ursa?" she asked sweetly.

"Lord, give me patience!" Alex groaned fervently.

"I'm sorry, Alex," she said between fits of laughter, "honestly I am."

"You certainly sound it," he snapped, not appreciating her humor. "Look, if you aren't interested in learning about the constellations, just say so, dammit, and put an end to your adolescent charade!"

His voice was sharp with disapproval. All too often in the past week he had either been on the verge of anger or openly hostile with her, and Eden felt perilously close to tears.

"I do want to learn about the stars," she protested shakily, attempting to placate him. "Please tell me about them."

He must have been convinced of her contrition because after a few minutes of pained silence he resumed pointing out various constellations and individual stars. Gradually his manner thawed, and he regained his earlier enthusiasm. Using Ursa Major as a landmark, he taught her how to locate Boötes and to identify Arcturus; then Gemini and its twin first-magnitude stars, Castor and Pollux. With these as a reference she quickly learned how to find Procyon, even brighter than the Twins.

Thanks to the lessons Lars Nilssen had given her, she already knew a few of the constellations: Draco —Alex was so testy, she was careful not to make the mistake of calling it the Dragon—Cassiopeia, and the Pleiades.

They lay head to head, like the spokes of a wheel, in their sleeping bags, for the temperature often dipped to near freezing even on summer nights at this altitude, and she listened more to the sound of his voice than to the sense of what he said as he told her some of the legends about the constellations. She fought back the threatening tears with plucky determination and watched the stars as they followed their courses across the sky. They looked distant and cold. As distant and cold as Alex was with her lately.

Eden sighed deeply and let her thoughts stray even further from Alex's lecture. It seemed that so far as he was concerned, she could no longer do anything right. He complained she never put things away properly and he couldn't find them when he wanted them. When she reacted by adopting a strict hands-off policy toward his belongings, he objected, because the cabin was so cluttered.

He'd gone back to working on his book in the loft instead of using the main room of the cabin, claiming her constant fidgeting interfered with his concentration. She especially resented the unfairness of that accusation because, while she knew she had some bad habits, she didn't fidget.

Yesterday he'd shouted at her about the way she was dressed, despite the fact that she wore perfectly respectable shorts and a halter top that was well-suited to the weather. He'd been wearing only shorts himself at the time, and when she had logically brought this to his attention, he'd resorted to his other prevailing mood and become remote and icily polite.

She sighed again. Since the day she had blacked out after their swim, the warm amiability that had once existed between them had been lost.

What's wrong with him? she wondered. Heaven knew, she had tried to behave as she always had with him.

She drew in another deep breath and was caught holding it when Alex threatened, "Red, if you sigh once more . . . just *one* more time"—he emphasized repressively—"I'm going to be sorely tempted to take drastic action to put a stop to it. Then you'll have genuine cause to feel sorry for yourself."

She lay on her back with one arm thrown across her forehead, hardly daring to exhale, not daring to move, and felt the tears well in her eyes and trickle unchecked down her cheeks. She exerted all her will to keep from making the smallest sound and was unaware that Alex had shifted position until his warm hand grasped her wrist and lifted her arm away from her face.

She looked up through her lashes and saw his face

poised above her. He released her wrist and his hand moved to her cheek, finding the dampness there.

"I'm sorry, Red," he said softly and began drying her tears with a gentle rain of kisses that closed her eyelids before they traced the salty tracks of the tears on her temples. His hand was tangled in her hair now, firmly anchoring her so that she could not pull away when his mouth found hers as lightly as when he'd kissed her at the lake, but when Eden tensed at even that feathery contact, he immediately drew back and looked down at her. His fingers tested the velvety skin of her throat.

What can he see in the darkness? she thought. She didn't close her eyes. She remained unresisting while he studied her face until at last she trembled under the impact of his scrutiny. Her pulse was racing beneath his knowing fingertips. She saw the white gleam of his teeth as he smiled briefly with satisfaction at what he'd discovered about her, and his hand trailed along the fine line of her jaw to cup her chin possessively, so that his easy grip caused her lips to purse.

This time she could not withstand the sensual onslaught of his kiss; for his mouth covered hers urgently, and as he teased the sweet contour of her lower lip with the tip of his tongue, the rigidity left her body and her mouth softened and finally opened for him, and it was as if nothing else existed. She was aware only of the deepening ardor of his kiss, of his tongue hotly exploring her mouth, igniting her own

*113*

response so that her entire being became focused on that one point of contact with him.

She was so dazed, she did not know he had moved until he lay beside her and unzipped her sleeping bag to draw her fully into his arms. A new dimension was added to the delights he was teaching her as his hands stroked deliberately down her back to her hips, pressing her closely against him; so closely that she was instantly aware of his arousal and knew a surge of inner pride that she could affect him as strongly as he affected her.

His lips searched the hollows of her throat, and she felt the moistness of his tongue as he tasted the sweetness there, and instinctively she wrapped her arms about him, her hands moving of their own volition to twine themselves in his hair, to caress his shoulders and back, to pull him even nearer to her as she bowed her body into the thrusting hardness of his.

It was not until she felt the chill of the night air on her skin that she realized he had removed her pajama top. But her disquiet was fleeting and rapidly dispelled as she was seared by the heat of his hands, delicately fondling and shaping the soft tender fullness of her breasts, by his mouth boldly seeking the sensitive nipples. Something inside her seemed to melt and yearn uncontrollably for him and the newness, the strangeness, the nearly overwhelming strength of this sensation was suddenly frightening to her.

She turned her head from side to side to escape the

hungry assault of his mouth and her body writhed, trying to dislodge the weight of his, but this only served to make her more conscious of the intimacy of his hold on her.

She panicked, and her hands gripped his shoulders so that her nails dug into his skin, pushing him away, pummeling him, fighting him.

"Red, honey, what's wrong?" Alex's husky voice seemed to come from far away.

"I can't," she cried hoarsely.

He abruptly rolled away so that he no longer touched her in any way; and though it was what she'd wanted, she felt he had rejected her with the promptness, the completeness, of his compliance to her wish.

"Oh, you *can* all right," he taunted her, coldly angry. "And you want to—don't try to tell yourself otherwise. What you mean is, you *won't.*" He laughed cruelly. "There's a very crude slang term for a little bitch like you—but it's less unpleasant than what you do to a man!"

"Please, you don't understand—" She tried to explain but was rendered mute by the hot lump of tears that had lodged in her throat, and Alex continued his denunciation of her as if she hadn't spoken at all.

"All you had to do was say no. There was no need to play the outraged virgin."

He looked at her, brutally appraising her, and something of her fear and embarrassment must have communicated itself to him—from her posture, from her hands that modestly clutched the flannel pajama top under her chin to cover her breasts—for he laughed again, mirthlessly, mockingly.

"My God," he exclaimed, "you *are* a virgin!" He shook his head with disbelief. "You should be in a museum, hermetically sealed in a glass case, not allowed to run free."

He got to his feet, and she heard him rearranging his own sleeping bag some distance away, sliding into it, and zipping it up.

She lay completely still, frozen by shame. He laughed with bitter amusement occasionally, and his ridicule added to her misery. Finally even his hollow laughter stopped, and after what seemed an eternity she moved restlessly, still gripped by unbearable tension.

"For God's sake, relax and go to sleep," he muttered. "You have nothing to fear from me." He yawned and jested derisively. "I make it a rule never to ravish maidens unless there's a full moon."

Though she longed for escape from her wretched self-contempt, Eden didn't sleep that night. She knew to the second when Alex fell asleep, and resentment swelled within her that, unlike her, he'd found a temporary respite from the awkwardness of their situation.

It was anger that rescued her from humiliation. Initially her rage was directed at Alex for his apparent duplicity: he'd told her that she was not physically appealing to him. Then it struck her that perhaps he hadn't been lying when he'd said that.

She sifted through her memories, trying to recall

what type of girl he'd found attractive ten years before. Most of the ones she'd seen him with had been tall, tanned, blond, and vapid but they'd each had about them an indefinable air of sultry sensuality that she'd recognized even at the uninformed age of twelve. They hadn't had much talent for dialogue, but then he'd spent no time at all talking with them in the green, vine-shadowed murkiness of the arbor.

The one who'd lasted longest with him had been Monica. In retrospect Eden decided Monica had given every indication of having been constructed of silicone from the neck down and of having nothing in her glamorous head but air. Monica's favorite conversational gambits had consisted of "Oh, yeah?," "But naturally!," and "Kiss me again, Alex." No doubt the last one accounted for Alex's relatively lengthy fascination with her—that and the improbably proportioned curves of her shapely body.

One indisputable fact emerged from her recollections of the girls Alex had found so attractive. In no way did Eden Lange Lassiter conform to the composite of their physical attributes.

From this, as well as from the uncaring way he'd behaved, from his marked lack of concern for her feelings, it was obvious that he was not emotionally involved with her. He'd wanted a woman, and she'd been the only one available. God, but she'd been available!

If she'd been more experienced with men, she would surely have recognized the danger signals he'd been emitting with his short-tempered outbursts for the past week and safely avoided the traumatizing outcome of tonight's events.

No, she contradicted herself with rueful honesty; if she'd been more knowledgeable, she'd never have called a halt to his lovemaking, and at this moment they'd be cozily sharing her sleeping bag—though it was unlikely they'd be doing much sleeping.

She should be deeply grateful that her innocence had prevented that from happening. Whatever transient pleasure Alex and she might have known together would have carried too high a penalty. The simple facade of their marriage would have been lost, and she would have found herself trapped in the double bind of love and marriage. It was bad enough that she loved Alex without the added fetter of being sexually enthralled by him.

She'd told Alex love usually didn't endure and she could only hope that this would prove to be true in her case; that what she felt for him would soon die a natural death for want of sustenance.

She told herself she should be feeling relief rather than suffering regret that she had allowed her fear of the risks that were implicit in loving Alex to overrule her compelling need for him, but she succeeded only in whipping up a cold anger at herself.

When the first rays of the sun pierced the fine mist that veiled the mountaintop, Alex awoke. He was depressingly bright-eyed and energetic as he climbed out of his sleeping bag and, with a total lack of self-consciousness for his state of near nudity in the khaki-colored bikini briefs that were all he wore, rolled up his bedding and stowed it away in his pack before he bothered to pull on his jeans and finish getting dressed.

He combed his hair with his fingers so that it stood on end in wild clusters and thoughtfully tested the overnight growth of stubble on his chin before he found his soap and towel and disappeared into the trees, heading for the small stream nearby to complete his morning ablutions.

When he returned a few minutes later, he looked only fractionally neater. He'd obviously doused his head thoroughly with water, for small droplets of it still sparkled in his dark hair. By rights he should have appeared less than his usual magnetically attractive self, but instead his disheveled appearance emphasized his rugged masculinity.

He saw Eden was awake and watching him. She looked as wan and fragile as she felt as she peered owlishly up at him from the warm nest of her bed. She sensed the beginnings of a headache behind her eyes, and her stomach churned with nausea.

"Rise and shine, Red," he called cheerfully.

She winced as the sound of his voice caused the incipient throbbing in her head to expand to the proportions of a boulder being rolled around inside her skull.

"Do you have to talk so loudly?" she whispered huskily, closing her eyes against the early-morning vitality of his grin and adding vehemently, "I *hate* people who are so blasted chipper first thing in the morning!"

119

"Come on, Sunshine," he coaxed as he ruthlessly pulled her sleeping bag aside. She lay huddled and shivering in her flannel pajamas, which were childishly patterned with yellow rosebuds. "You'll feel better after you have some breakfast."

"I don't want anything to eat," she protested through clenched teeth. Her stomach heaved at the thought of food.

"Coffee, then," he offered in apparent sympathy, then spoiled the effect by observing with inhumane glee as she grabbed up her clothes and staggered into the woods, tender-footed in her shoeless state, "God, Red, you really do look terrible!"

By the time they arrived back at the cabin, it was almost noon, and Eden's headache was firmly entrenched. She went directly to her room without excusing herself. Blinded by the severity of the pressure in her head, she groped for the tablets her doctor had prescribed and took the recommended dosage before she drew the blinds and crawled into the welcome haven of her bed. She didn't bother to turn back the covers or undress.

For a time she was inundated by the pain, then gradually the medicine took hold, and she dozed fitfully through the afternoon. She could tell it was evening by the change of light in her room when Alex came in to check on her. She was aware of him moving about and opened her eyes to see him beside the bed.

"You all right, Red?" He whispered the question so he wouldn't disturb her if she was still asleep.

"Headache," she mumbled. The palliative effect of the medicine had worn off, and the pain was worse than before. She stirred as her mouth filled with the metallic, salty taste of nausea.

"Oh, God," she moaned, "I'm going to be sick."

Alex picked her up as though she were weightless and carried her to the bathroom. He exhibited welcome sensitivity to her discomfiture by waiting outside until the sounds of her retching abated. When he lifted her in his arms again, she resisted momentarily.

"I can walk," she protested feebly.

"I know you can," he acknowledged easily, "but I like to carry you, so humor me."

He set her on her feet in her bedroom.

"Let's get you out of those clothes," he ordered, and impersonally proceeded to help her divest herself of her T-shirt and denim slacks, easing the latter over her shoes while she sat on the edge of the bed, clad only in her bra and panties. He knelt beside her and untied her boots and pulled them off, then her socks. She held her head in her hands, incapable of offering any further opposition to his aid.

Alex had seen the pill bottle on her nightstand. As he stood her on her feet and folded the blankets back for her, he asked, "Are you due to take more of your medicine?"

"Yes." She subsided onto the bed.

He left the room and returned a few seconds later

with a glass of water. Shaking out two of the tablets, he gave them to her with the water, then eased her back onto her pillows and tucked the covers under her chin with unexpected tenderness. He smoothed her hair back from her forehead and his hand lingered, savoring the silky fineness of it between his fingers.

"Can I get you anything else?"

"No," she breathed. His hand was soothing as he stroked her forehead.

"Does this help?" he asked, referring to the massaging motion of his hand.

"Ummm." What helped most was his care of her, his being there.

Alex continued the rhythmic stroking, feeling her relax under his touch, until the evenness of her breathing told him she slept. He straightened and stood looking down at her. He could barely see her face in the gathering darkness and leaned closer, marveling at the vulnerable cast of her features.

He realized he had never really looked at her as she was now, completely relaxed and unguarded. If he had, he never would have questioned her innocence. His eyes traveled over the outline of her body, noting the slight but unmistakably feminine mound she created beneath the covers.

She was such a bundle of contradictions, so thorny and spirited, he'd been startled to realize how small she actually was when he'd lifted her in his arms and discovered her to be featherlight and fine-boned.

Feeling uniquely protective, he kissed her lightly on the forehead before he left the room.

## Chapter Eight

She felt as if she'd slept for a year, although it was only noon of the following day when she wandered into the main room. Her head was still slightly tender and muzzy from the medicine, but she knew from experience she was on the mend.

Alex was working with the rough draft of his book at an occasional table he'd moved to the front of the couch and when he looked up at her, it suddenly occurred to her to wonder how she would be received by him.

"You could stand some coffee, I think," he suggested mildly, "and something to eat."

Eden began to move shakily toward the kitchen, but he waylaid her.

"I'll get it for you," he said.

He seated her in the chair opposite the sofa and wrapped the Navaho blanket around her.

Does this mean all is forgiven, and we're to resume being friends? she asked herself, but she was too weak and hungry to contemplate the question any further. She sat numbly, looking out of the windows at the sunlit panorama of lake, trees, mountain, and sky until Alex returned with a tray for her.

He went back to his editing, and she watched the changing moods displayed on his face instead of the scene outdoors as she ate her scrambled eggs and toast and sipped her coffee. He'd opened a can of mandarin orange segments as a special treat for her.

She was mesmerized by his reactions, dramatically exhibited in his expression, as he reviewed his writing; one minute scowling, the next, smiling, his face fierce or tender by turns.

He sensed she was studying him, glanced at her, and grinned. She smiled back at him tentatively.

"You look a little better now," he observed.

"Thank you. I feel much better. And thank you for being so kind yesterday."

He shrugged.

"I'm not very brave about pain," she ventured. "That's one of the things I admire in your mother."

"Yes. In her unassuming way she's truly phenomenal." He looked at Eden with narrowed eyes as though measuring the possibility that she was fishing for compliments. "But I disagree with your assessment of your own courage. You weren't half bad last night."

Eden peered into the dregs of the coffee in her cup and did not respond to his faint praise.

"Have you seen your own mother lately?"

The question was entirely unexpected, and she started.

"No," she replied evenly enough. "I haven't seen Florence for years. She's remarried, you know, and living in Los Angeles."

"You don't seem to resent her abandonment of you," he remarked.

"Well, it's just that I recognize that she has her limitations. To be honest, I did resent the way she behaved toward my father and Elaine, but I never had to rely on her, and I never expected her to take any maternal interest in me—to act like a mother is supposed to act. It's not entirely her fault. She was raised to be a butterfly, and one doesn't expect a butterfly to serve any purpose other than to be decorative."

"And harvest the nectar of life," Alex added.

"Exactly."

"Yet some butterflies are amazingly tough, Red. For all their gossamer appearance, their wings are capable of carrying them on annual migrations of thousands of miles."

"I'll admit that Florence has her own brand of toughness, but it's derived basically from weakness rather than strength. She doesn't concern herself with anyone but herself."

"I'm surprised you're so philosophical about her.

You really don't appear to harbor any bitterness toward her."

"It would be senseless to hold her responsible." A spasm of anger touched her fine features, and her voice hardened uncompromisingly as she confided further. "The resentment I feel is toward Frank and Justine for their treatment of my mother."

"Surely Florence reached the age, as we all do," Alex argued, "where she was free to choose the kind of woman she wanted to be."

"Yes, but if their upbringing of Elaine was a fair example of the way they'd dealt with my mother, she was terribly ill-equipped to make the simplest of decisions, let alone such an important one as that."

Alex grinned again, lightening the mood between them.

"I just recalled the first time I saw you," he reminisced. "It was the spring you first came to live next door, so you must have been about ten. I was trimming the hedge by the drive one afternoon when I noticed Elaine and you coming up the lane on your way home from a birthday party.

"Your dress was bedraggled, the hem was torn and half coming down, your hair was straggling out of its ribbons, you were so smeared with party refreshments, you looked like a walking menu—and you'd obviously had a wonderful time—while Elaine looked as though she'd just stepped out of a bandbox.

"It had rained early in the day and she was just ahead of you, picking her way fastidiously to avoid spattering herself with mud, and all at once you

127

began stepping in every puddle you passed, more and more energetically, until finally you were jumping into them with both feet. And all the while you were coaxing Elaine to try it too. You were close to tears and pleading with her to loosen up and enjoy herself.

"But she just kept on walking with her haughty little nose in the air. Then she turned in at your uncle's drive, and you stood in a particularly deep puddle with water nearly up to your knees, brushing at the stains on your party dress, and this expression of acute disgust suddenly appeared on your face." He laughed. "God! You were a sight!"

"I remember." Eden shuddered with distaste. "I didn't really like being all muddy. It's slimy, icky stuff."

"I called to you," Alex reminded her, "but you ran away."

She envisioned him as he had been that day when he had appeared, seemingly from out of nowhere, tall and authoritative, dark and handsome. He had been an awesome and compellingly romantic figure to her at ten. Now she was more than twice that age but, without even trying, he still made the same impression on her.

"You looked so—forbidding, I guess," she finally explained. "I thought you believed my efforts were directed at getting Elaine into trouble and that you wanted to scold me."

"No," he revealed. "I was going to take you to my mother so she could help you clean up—destroy the evidence so you wouldn't be punished when you got home. I could tell you were only trying—at no small expense to yourself—to tempt Elaine into kicking over the traces and experiencing something new."

"I was never successful though." She smiled ruefully.

His expression ironic, Alex retorted, "Do you mean to say you've finally given up trying to smooth your sister's path for her?"

Stung by his censure, Eden averted her head and didn't respond to his accusation.

"That's one trait you've inherited from your father," Alex went on. "The quixotic inclination to take on lost causes." He sounded irritated. "Jonathan would have been very proud of you."

Eden's head snapped up in surprise. "I didn't realize you knew my father."

"He spoke to the English class a few times when I was in high school, though I'll admit that this particular judgment is based on hearsay."

"Why are you so—" Eden hesitated and Alex intervened.

"Angry?" he supplied. When she nodded, he exclaimed hotly, "Because as a little girl you were burdened with adult worries and responsibilities by the very people who should have been cherishing you."

He walked with supple, athletic grace to where she sat and, placing a hand on each arm of the chair, leaned over until his forehead rested against hers. She could see warm gold flecks dancing in his dark brown eyes.

"You're a rare, intrepid, obstinate little butterfly, Red."

"And I should be locked in a glass case," she rejoined tensely.

"No, I've changed my mind about that." The laugh lines fanned out from his eyes as he smiled, wickedly enticing. "What you should do is get rid of your—chrysalis." His voice was low and purposely seductive, leaving her in no doubt that the word *virginity* should be substituted for *chrysalis.*

"Unless you do," he warned her with mock solemnity, "you'll never know what it is to taste the sweetness of the nectar and fly free in the sunlight."

"I'll never have my wings singed either," she parried tartly, "or find myself pinned to somebody's specimen board while they go off chasing after some other butterfly."

"Ah, Red, you misjudge me!"

He acted the clown, lithely going down on one knee in front of her, his hand over his heart, his face woeful, trying to look as though he were mortally offended.

"I wasn't suggesting you should enlist in anyone's collection. What you need is a connoisseur who wants one perfect, passionate little butterfly who doesn't roam from flower to flower."

He looked so ridiculous, she burst out laughing, and smiling with satisfaction Alex got to his feet and touched the dimple in her cheek with his fingertip.

"That's better," he said softly, and bending down,

he replaced the touch of his finger with his lips, briefly and undemanding.

"Am I forgiven for the other night?" He looked at her quizzically.

"Yes," she smiled. "Am I?"

He nodded. "After that performance, need you ask?"

"May I ask another question?"

Again he nodded.

"Whatever happened to Monica?"

He appeared to be puzzled and responded blankly, "Monica who?"

As one hot summer day followed another, Eden found that the requirement of keeping the daily diary provided her with a much needed safety valve. She completely lost her reservations about revealing her thoughts and emotions for future review by strangers and looked upon her journal as a trusted confidant who would never judge her, harshly or otherwise, no matter what secrets she told it.

It was especially helpful with regard to her feelings for Alex, as this outlet made it possible for her to maintain her fond attitude toward him without permitting him to guess the ardent depth of the love he'd inspired. Contrary to her hopes, her love for him showed no signs of dying with the passage of the summer but grew until she could scarcely contain it.

If there had been no necessity for the almost constant pretense, their isolation would have been idyllic so far as she was concerned. Under the circumstances, however, it seemed at first a welcome relief when they had a visitor.

It was near the end of August when he materialized out of the dusk one evening, looking like a refugee from a Western movie as he approached the cabin, bandy-legged and grizzled, trailing two pack-laden burros behind him. Eden and Alex watched him from the deck, where they were preparing to eat dinner, as he came nearer.

"Do you see what I see?" Alex asked, his expression incredulous.

"I see it," Eden replied breathlessly, "but I'm not sure I believe it." She leaped to her feet suddenly and was nearly dancing with excitement as she cried, "Oh, Alex, won't it be wonderful to see someone else? Do you think he'll stay awhile?"

"Take it easy, Red," Alex cautioned softly. "We're a long way from civilization and we don't know this character from Adam."

Eden's face fell with disappointment. "Can we at least ask him to stay overnight?"

"We'll see," he replied noncommittally.

He stood close beside her, wrapping his arm about her waist and letting his hand rest with easy intimacy on her hipbone. She looked up at him quickly, surprised by this unaccustomed familiarity.

"Follow my lead," he whispered before turning to observe the man who was by now nearing the stairs to the deck.

The man stopped a few yards away, still hanging on to the halter with which he led his burros, and swept his dust-caked hat off his head, partially crushing the age-worn felt in one grimy hand. He was not very tall and was sharp-featured, thin, and leathery-looking. The fringe of oily gray hair that ringed his balding head was long and ill-kempt, shaggily trimmed, as was his beard. He looked at them from beneath his bushy dark eyebrows and, with the ingratiating smile he offered Alex, revealed he was almost toothless.

"Evenin' mister," he called in his grating voice. "Missus."

His attention shifted to Eden, and she felt his look crawling over her, lingering with lascivious interest on the soft curves of her breasts and the gentle swell of her hips. She moved closer to Alex and felt his arm tighten about her in the same instant. He grew more vigilant as he confronted the man and he didn't return his greeting.

"Name's Sam Parkins, and this here's Sally and Junebug," he cackled rustily as he introduced his moth-eaten animals. "I been prospectin' hereabouts for some time now. Ain't seen hide nor hair of another livin' person in a dog's age. You two sure are a sight for sore eyes!"

He transferred his hat to the hand that held the burros and extended his free hand toward Alex.

"Alex Lassiter," Alex replied tersely but in an even tone that belied his instinctive distrust of the stranger. "This is my wife." He didn't mention Eden's name and he ignored the man's outstretched hand.

133

There ensued a moment's strained silence before Sam cackled again and remarked hopefully, "That fish smells mighty good, missus. Trout, ain't it?"

Alex answered quickly, before Eden could respond. "That it is." He spoke to Eden without taking his eyes off of Sam. "Fix him a plate, honey."

Before he removed his arm from her waist, he gave her a heartening squeeze. She moved reluctantly away from him to do as he'd requested.

"You been here long?" Sam asked.

"Since June."

"When I pass this way, I most always camp down by the lake."

Alex inclined his head. "You're welcome to stay there for tonight." He stressed the time limitation.

The two men continued to watch each other with wary intensity. Eden hurriedly brought Sam's dinner plate, then stood irresolutely, not knowing where to deliver it. With a barely perceptible nod of his head Alex indicated she should leave it on the steps to the porch and she did so, uncomfortably aware of Sam's covert stare following her every movement. She wished she were wearing something less revealing than her abbreviated shorts and sun top.

She scurried back to the security of Alex's side, grateful for the support of his arm about her.

Sam jammed his disreputable hat back on his head and with surprising agility moved forward to retrieve the plate. He seemed to exude a malevolence as strong as the musky body odor that permeated the air about him. Stepping back a ways, he observed them, silently irate, for a time before he said with deceptive courtesy, "Thanks, ma'am." He touched the drooping brim of his hat with a gnarled forefinger. "Mister,"

He turned on his heel and called obscenities to his pack animals to get them moving as he set off down the trail to the lake.

They watched him until he was hidden by the trees. Even then, Alex continued peering keenly into the darkness of the forest as though to be certain Sam had not doubled back. As her own concern lessened a bit Eden realized that his fingers grasped her so tightly that it was painful. She tried to ease away and his grip increased.

"Alex," she gasped.

He looked down at her absently.

"You're hurting me."

"Sorry about that, Red." He grinned sheepishly. Then he suggested, "Let's finish eating inside."

Eden agreed with alacrity and together they carried their dinner things into the kitchen. Once inside, Alex bolted the doors before joining Eden at the table. Neither of them was very hungry, and Alex was so immersed in thought that Eden didn't disturb him, though she longed to pour out her disappointment that their visitor was so unsavory, and her fear of his being essentially evil.

Instead she occupied herself with preparing a pot of coffee. When she offered Alex his cup, he accepted it and drank it without breaking the silence between them. It wasn't till he'd poured a second cup for himself that he spoke.

"Don't go outside alone tonight, Red. I'll escort you to the bathroom and back."

She shivered suddenly, wondering why she should still feel so threatened. She was safely inside their snug cabin, and Alex, she knew, could break Sam in two if the need arose.

Never had time passed so slowly as it did that evening. Eden jumped anxiously at the slightest noise and dreaded the time when she would have to retire to the solitary confinement of her room. Alex appeared relaxed as he sprawled in the chair with a book open on his lap, but she noticed he seldom turned a page.

Finally the fire burned down until the foundation log collapsed with a loud cracking sound, sending a shower of sparks up the chimney. Soon only embers and ashes remained and Alex announced it was time to turn in.

He accompanied her to the bathroom and waited outside the door as she perfunctorily washed, and cleaned her teeth. As they reentered the kitchen Eden's diminished pride vanished totally. Her courage had been shattered the moment she'd got a good look at Sam.

"Alex," she quavered, not looking at him, "I'm afraid to stay alone in my room tonight."

His arm went around her, and as he felt her tremble he held her close. She felt secure enough like that and sighed with relief at the immediate easing of her tension. She leaned against him, relishing his strength, and wrapped her arms about his narrow waist, linking her hands behind him. He stroked her hair, and his breath stirred it lightly as he murmured, "It's all right, Red. We'll both sleep in your room."

She was so frightened that she eagerly acceded to this plan and she found herself installed in the top-bunk bed with a minimum of fuss. She got into her pajamas while Alex took his turn in the bathroom and checked the doors and windows. When he came into the room, she was safely under the covers.

She lay on her side, facing the wall, and listened to the faint rustling sounds that indicated he was undressing; heard the thud of his boots on the floor as he discarded them, the sharp chink of his belt buckle. He put out the lantern, and she heard him climb into the bottom bunk.

She still felt an illogical terror, and her body was clenched and aching. Her heart was pounding so loudly, she was afraid Alex would hear it. She willed herself to relax and grow drowsy but remained wide-awake.

Alex was breathing evenly and deeply; she thought she would concentrate on that regular, reassuring sound and try to synchronize her own respirations to his, but the attempt to inhale and exhale to a pattern that was unnatural to her only made her more tense.

She shifted about from time to time minutely, in an effort to be as quiet as possible, trying to find a position that was both comfortable and sleep-inducing. She wished they could talk about something—

anything that would take her mind off her nameless fears and her physical unease.

At last, disgruntled, Alex complained gruffly, "Dammit, Red, can't you settle down? Sharing a bed with you must be like sleeping with a bagful of snakes!"

"I—I'm sorry," she apologized stiltedly.

"You fidget more than anyone I've ever known," he persisted unjustly.

"I do not fidget," she objected hotly, then added, "At least I don't usually." She was dismayed to hear the plaintive note in her voice.

He laughed softly.

"What's so funny?" she snapped. If he were to make fun of her now, it would be more than she could take.

"You are." He sounded unexpectedly serious after his apparent amusement at her expense.

She moved again, and the springs of her bed protested loudly. She heard Alex utter an epithet under his breath.

"Since it looks as if neither of us is going to get any sleep for a while," he said with patient forbearance, "why don't you tell me why you're so frightened of sex."

"This isn't the time or the place for such a discussion," she objected weakly.

"Oh, but it is. We have all night, nowhere to go, and with you so unwilling, nothing better to do."

Eden turned onto her back carefully, in an unsuccessful effort to conceal this additional movement.

"It's not sex I'm afraid of," she said after a long constrained silence. "At least not sex, per se."

"What is it, then?"

"You ought to know. You're the one who defined it so concisely."

"You're afraid of falling in love," he said softly. "Of being hurt."

She remained silent, not trusting her voice if she were to reply.

"Do you really believe not loving will protect you from harm?"

"I don't know," she admitted huskily. "But from what I've seen it do to people, it seems a lot safer than the alternative."

"You'd like to be convinced you're wrong," he stated with arrogant confidence. "I can't guarantee I can do that, but I'm going to tell you about something that happened to some friends of mine."

The vibrant timbre of Alex's voice was solace in itself, and Eden's tension dissipated rapidly as she became engrossed in the story he related.

"My friends had been happily married for quite a few years. They had a lovely home, a son they were proud of, and a deeply satisfying family life together. Then they had another baby—another boy—only this one was severely retarded."

Alex paused briefly, and she heard him sigh before he continued his narrative.

"No one knew what had gone wrong. Probably it was just that the mother was well into her thirties, and that increases the risks of such birth defects occurring. This was quite a few years ago, and attitudes were different then. My friends were urged to put the baby in an institution and go on about their lives, but they couldn't bring themselves to do that. He was their son, not some kind of toy to be cast aside because it didn't function properly, and they wanted him with them.

"In the end they ignored all the well-meaning advice and took him home. They worked with him and loved him, and he made miraculous progress and grew to know and love them. Because above all else they were wise and loving people, they also saw to it that their older son didn't feel shunted aside or of no further importance to them, but made sure that he was involved as well, and caring for this baby became a beautiful, meaningful experience for all of them.

"The baby lived only a little more than two years and when he died, people said it was a blessing because he'd have been a lifelong burden to his family and he'd never have been capable of leading a normal life. My friends didn't feel that way at all. They felt they'd been blessed by having him because he'd brought them so much love, he'd brought them closer as a family, he'd given them the unique opportunity to care for someone unselfishly and to grow in understanding."

Alex was silent for a time, and his voice was husky as he concluded. "His mother once told me that while she'd certainly never have chosen to have had a child with such a severe problem—only to suffer the grief of losing him after such a short time—she had no regrets about having had that very special child. She said that when all the sorrow was balanced against all the happiness, even if the sorrow weighed more heavily, she could never bring herself to forfeit having experienced the joy."

Eden listened with an intentness that approached reverence as Alex finished speaking, and she was reluctant to break the almost worshipful silence that filled the room. She felt small and humbled for having been so preoccupied with a problem as trivial as hers, when by comparison his friends had confronted great personal tragedy with valiant grace of spirit and selfless generosity.

The message that Alex had intended her to receive was obvious, and her thoughts turned to her father. Had Jonathan also found that the joy was worth the pain? What pleasure had he derived from loving her mother? He'd had slightly less than a year of a tempestuous marriage with—she had no doubt—its own moments of ecstasy. Was that sufficient compensation for the ten years he'd been deprived of the object of his adoration? And, she added belatedly, he'd had her. Had she been a source of joy that overshadowed the pain?

If she were to follow her own desires and give physical expression to her love for Alex, she would at least know the meaning of the fulfillment of her need for him.

How much time remained of their summer together? The time had passed so swiftly. Could it really be that only three weeks were left? She had no illusions that Alex would still want her when the summer was over. Was it humanly possible to love enough in three weeks to last a lifetime? But if she were to have a child, Alex's child . . .

"Red," Alex's voice called her back from her soul-searching, "have you reached a verdict?"

"I—I'm not sure." Her uncertainty was clearly registered in her voice. Then she asked, "The friends you told me about, Alex, are they—"

She couldn't finish her query, but he confirmed her suspicions, acknowledging simply, "My parents."

## Chapter Nine

The campsite on the beach appeared to be deserted. From the window in the loft Eden scanned the stretches of the path to the lake that were visible through the trees and, seeing no trace of Sam Parkins, decided it would be silly to waken Alex to escort her to the bath. Their unwelcome guest had probably left at first light. She looked again at the beach and with the aid of Alex's binoculars she could clearly see the remnants of Sam's campfire. It looked as though it had been doused hours before.

She packed the binoculars away in their case and climbed down the ladder from the loft. It was nearly nine o'clock, and she'd been awake since shortly after dawn, despite the fact they'd talked until the early hours of the morning.

She entered the bedroom stealthily and collected

some clean clothes to put on after her shower. Although it was early in the day, it was already hot, and she felt sticky and uncomfortable in her flannel pajamas.

Alex appeared to be deeply asleep, lying on his back with one arm flung above his head and the other hanging limply over the edge of the mattress. He'd kicked the blankets off and was covered only by the sheet that was tangled about his hips, barely preserving decency. The whiteness of the sheet emphasized the deeply tanned skin on the flat plain of his belly, the darkness of the mat of curly hair on his chest. It was fortunate the loft contained a full-size bed, for he was much too big to have spent the night comfortably in the small confines of the bunk bed. His feet stuck out beyond the end of it, and the breadth of his shoulders all but filled its entire width.

His face was troubled, even in repose, and Eden wanted desperately to smooth the worry lines on his forehead with her fingertips. His hair had grown even longer and curled more wildly than ever; the only thing about him that was uncontrolled, she thought. She smiled tenderly as she looked down at him. She hadn't the heart to disturb his much needed rest just so she would have an unnecessary guard to see her to the bath.

She left the room quietly and, with her step quickened by anticipation, moved through the kitchen to let herself out of the cabin. It was only a few paces to the bathroom, and she paused for a moment outside the door with the morning sun hot on her uplifted face as she breathed in the piny fragrance of the air.

She was totally unprepared for the hand that was speedily clamped, with suffocating pressure, over her mouth and nose, the arms that grasped her with frightening strength, pinning one of her arms uselessly at her side. She caught the stench of Sam's unwashed body, and her eyes were white-rimmed with horror as she instinctively fought to break free of his hold on her.

She reached behind her with her free hand and tried to grab a handful of his hair, tried to scratch and gouge at his eyes, but he caught hold of her wrist and twisted that arm behind her at an angle so painful that tears spurted from her eyes. And all the while he was relentlessly dragging her farther from the sanctuary of the cabin into the trees.

She bucked and strained with all her strength to escape as he pressed her close to him to keep her arms imprisoned against his scrawny chest, freeing his hand to probe roughly at her breasts. Though his assessing fingers bit deeply into her soft flesh, her terror was such that she felt no pain.

He laughed maniacally, and his fetid breath caused a burning nausea to rise within her as he said, "Well, girlie, you're worth the waitin' for."

His fingers were clawing at her pajamas, and his frenzied concentration on that allowed her enough room to jab her elbow sharply into his stomach. He grunted and doubled over a bit but recovered quickly; she was held more securely than ever as he grabbed a handful of her hair and tugged it cruelly, pulling her head back to rest on his shoulder.

"Little vixen, ain't you? Like to play rough," he muttered menacingly. "Well, I'm just the man to oblige you, girlie."

*Dear God,* she thought, *this can't be happening to me.* She was struggling silently, aware she was fast losing consciousness from his restrictive hold on her, despairing of overcoming the hideous strength contained in his stringy body, when suddenly she was freed. Her knees buckled and she collapsed onto the ground, holding her throat as she gasped for breath.

She was only hazily aware of the uneven battle that ensued between Alex and Sam. Her mind vaguely registered the thudding sound of blows, the high-pitched whistling of Sam's labored breathing, his moans of pain, and finally Alex's voice, thundering ominously with command, like an avenging angel.

"Get out of here, Parkins," he roared. "If I ever see you again, I swear, I'll kill you!"

Eden was sobbing with relief as Alex adjusted her clothing and carried her back to the cabin. She wrapped her arms tightly about his neck and buried her face in his shoulder and was loath to release her stranglehold on him when they reached the main room.

He had forcibly to pry her arms away as he muttered breathlessly, "God, Red, you're choking me!"

"I'm sorry," she cried. "I'm so sorry."

He put her down on the couch and she curled

her body protectively and sat hunched over, rocking slightly to and fro.

"You should be sorry," he said, scolding her as though she were a child. "I told you not to go outdoors without me. God! I was worried out of my skull when I woke up and found you were gone!"

She looked up at him through the prisms of the tears that shimmered in her eyes, and he seemed to loom over her, wrapped in rainbows.

"I'm sorry," she reiterated brokenly. "I'm sorry."

Alex knelt in front of her, and his face was grim as he surveyed her injuries. She was white with shock and she had long, livid welts on her hands and arms and on what he could see of her chest and shoulders. There was a deep scratch on her forearm where Sam had broken the skin and drawn blood, and another, only partially visible, that seemed to extend across the topmost curves of her breasts. Her lips were bruised and swollen and there was a small cut on her lower lip.

He reached out to touch a darkening bruise on her cheek, and she flinched and shrank away from him.

"No," she moaned, near hysteria. "Don't touch me!"

"It's all right, Red." He offered reassurance so calmly, she believed him. "Can I get you anything?"

"I—I just want to wash. I feel so dirty."

His breath caught in his throat and his brows drew together. The color drained from his face so that he was pasty white under his tan.

"Sam didn't—"

She shook her head in violent denial. Her eyes were tightly closed as though she were striving to erase the memory.

"He only touched me," she said. Her trembling hands indicated her breasts.

Alex exhaled in a long sigh. "Come along, then." He helped her to her feet and gently guided her toward the kitchen. "You can have a shower. I'll keep watch outside."

"Do you think he's still around?" Her eyes widened with alarm.

"No," he answered brusquely, "I think we've seen the last of him. But we won't take any chances till I'm positive."

It was not until she had showered and dressed that Eden noticed Alex's blood-stained shirt. He was spreading antiseptic on her scratches, and as she watched his dexterous application of the medicine, she saw that his knuckles were torn and swollen.

"Were you hurt?" she asked, forcing the question past the lump in her throat that was caused by her concern.

"This is all his," he referred to the blood. He flexed his fingers gingerly. "My hand is a little sore," he smiled grimly, "but it was worth it."

Eden caught his hand with both of hers, carried it to her lips, and placed a soft kiss on each of his damaged knuckles. When she released his hand and glanced up at him, she was amazed to see that he looked disconcerted.

"I just wanted to thank you properly," she explained as she smiled timorously at him.

"When you're feeling more yourself," he said dryly, "remind me to say a proper you're welcome."

Although she had slept very little the night before, Eden had trouble falling asleep that night. Her body cried out for rest, but every time she closed her eyes, she saw—as if in a nightmare—Parkins's leering face and felt swamped once again by the helpless, hopeless terror of the morning. She tossed and turned for what seemed like eons before she got into her fleecy robe and left her room, thinking that a hot drink might help her to relax.

As she waited for the water to heat for her cocoa, she realized it was not mental unease alone that was preventing her from sleeping, but physical discomfort as well. She was a solid mass of throbbing bruises that were now coming into full bloom, their garish blues, greens, and magentas relieved by the network of scratches and abrasions Parkins had inflicted, each of which stung and burned with individual fire.

"Red." Alex's soft voice as he stood sleep-rumpled in the kitchen doorway came as a complete surprise, and she started, spilling some of the boiling water she was adding to the cocoa mixture in her cup. "Can't you sleep?"

She shook her head, busily mopping the steaming puddle on the counter with a dishcloth to conceal the depth of her gratitude for his unexpected presence.

"I thought some cocoa might help," she explained. "Would you like some?"

"That sounds good."

He seated himself at the table, and she was aware that he followed each of her movements with his eyes as she took another mug from the cupboard, emptied a packet of the mix into it, and added hot water, stirring the resulting chocolate drink until it was smooth and creamy. She carried both cups to the table and sat in her usual chair opposite him.

"Thanks." Alex sampled his, still watching her. "There are some mild sedatives in the first-aid kit. I'll get one for you if you'd like me to."

"I'd rather not," she declined. Her voice was a small, tight whisper, as if even her vocal cords were tense.

"I checked around outside thoroughly, you know," Alex reminded her. "Parkins must be miles away by now."

"I know," she agreed in a murmur.

Lifting her eyes from her cocoa, she glanced up at him. He sat astride his chair with his arms folded across the back of it. He'd pulled on his Levi's jeans, some buckskin moccasins, and a red-plaid wool shirt that he hadn't taken the time to button.

"Could we just talk for a while?" she asked.

"What would you like to talk about?"

She floundered momentarily, mentally seeking a topic. "Would you tell me how you became interested in genetic research?"

"Initially it was because of my brother," Alex replied. "He died when I was fifteen, so I was old enough to appreciate fully the stress and grief his birth defect had caused my parents."

He paused to sip his cocoa, and Eden nodded, her face solemn.

"It's pure corn," he continued, "but I was at the age when idealism was beginning to rear its head, and when my father suddenly died the following spring, I resolved to find the specific cause for the syndrome my brother had suffered from and—well, sort of lay the solution at my mother's feet as an offering to alleviate her pain."

"It's not corny at all," Eden exclaimed. "I can easily understand why you'd want to do that for Paula." Shyly she confided, "When I was a little girl, I sometimes used to pretend that she was my mother."

"That's quite a coincidence," Alex remarked evenly, "because when you were a little girl, Mother used to wish you were her daughter."

Eden studied him closely but she could detect no sign that he was teasing her.

"Honestly?" she asked wistfully.

"Word of honor," Alex said. He held up one hand as though he were giving sworn testimony. "She used to watch for you to pass the house on your way home from school every day. You wore a red coat with a hood and you'd be singing at the top of your lungs." He chuckled at the recollection. "Mother said it was impossible not to be cheered up by you—even though you apparently couldn't sing any better then than you do now. She said anyone who could sing like that on their way to Frank and Justine's must have an unquenchable spirit."

"I wish I'd known," Eden said softly.

"Since I was away at college, I was grateful Mother had you to occupy her." Alex grinned meaningfully. "But I must admit, I'm happy you're not my sister."

Eden ducked her head and hastily changed the subject. "What happened after you made your resolution?" she asked.

Looking at him from beneath her lashes, she saw that his smile was twisted with self-mockery.

"I'd never been much of a student to that point. In fact, school had been one huge bore, and I was more of a hell-raiser than a scholar. When I made my decision, I was motivated enough to turn over a new leaf and apply myself to my classes, but at that time it was still only a means to an end. All I wanted was to earn grades that would assure my admission to a good university.

"It wasn't until I was well into my third year at Cal Tech that I developed the more positive attitude of studying for the sake of learning all that I was capable of. That was when I found myself getting sidetracked into my present field. It was especially intriguing, and I became more and more involved with it until finally my interest in it precluded even my original plan."

"It must be fascinating—almost like playing

God," Eden mused, "to develop a whole new organism."

"People do it every day, Red," Alex replied, "and have more fun in the creative process besides." When she looked at him, clearly wondering what he meant, he added dryly, "When they make babies."

She felt her cheeks growing warm at his teasing but maintained her equanimity well enough to ask, "Would you like to have children someday?"

"Why, Red!" he exclaimed, grinning broadly, purposely misunderstanding her. "Is that an invitation? If so, the answer is yes."

Her face was stinging now with the heat of her blush. "I was only curious." She gulped as she lifted one trembling hand and placed it on her cheek so as to cool it. The long sleeve of her robe fell away from her forearm as she did so, revealing the severe discoloration of her bruises.

Alex reached across the table and gently tugged her hand away from her face, rotating it and noting the extensiveness of her injuries. The broken, jagged wheals were inflamed and angry-looking. She tingled as though with electric shock at the sensations his touch generated, and her stomach muscles contracted when his thumb stroked repeatedly over the soft, sensitive skin of her inner wrist.

"Did you put more antiseptic on your scratches?" he asked thickly. His eyes were soft and unfocused when he raised them to hers.

Rendered drugged and mindless by his actions,

she was incapable of speech and nodded jerkily. Inside she was crying, *God, what is he doing to me?*

The spell was broken when he let go of her hand, frowning and shaking his head as if to clear it. He drained his cup and all but slammed it down on the table.

"I don't know about you," he stated coolly, "but I'm going back to bed."

Several days later the water system stopped functioning, tapering off until only the suggestion of a trickle came through the kitchen tap. This had happened a number of times before; when the water level dropped so low that the pipe was not submerged, or when the filter that kept debris from entering the pipeline itself had become clogged with pine needles, leaves, and twigs.

They had scouted the region about the cabin daily and had seen no sign that Sam Parkins was still in the neighborhood, but Eden still felt nervous about remaining alone for any length of time, even in the locked cabin, and accompanied Alex as he followed the route of the pipeline to the spring from which their water originated.

After a few hundred yards cross-country they paralleled the course of a rocky creek bed that drained the runoff from the spring into the lake. While it was obvious that, early in the season, the creek ran bank-full from the thaw, it was almost dry at this time of the year.

They talked as they hiked toward the spring. It

turned out that Alex recalled Monica after all, though it took Eden's description of her to jog his memory.

"Do you always remember your former girl friends by their measurements?" she teased lightly, hiding a twinge of jealousy.

"Not always," he rejoined reasonably. "It's just that hers were so—spectacular." His smile was beatific as he envisioned Monica's generous curves. "They were far and away her most prominent features."

Eden almost asked what he considered to be her own most prominent features, but stopped short of that when she thought of his nicknames for her. *"Red hair and freckles."* That was the description that would stimulate his remembrance of her years from now. Instead, she inquired, "What is Monica doing now?"

"She's married, and the last I heard, she had several children."

So she had not been *all* silicone!

"Does she still live in Eureka?"

"No. Somewhere in Marin County." He stopped walking and reached back in order to help her clamber over a particularly big boulder that blocked their trail. "Why all the interest in Monica?"

"No special reason," she answered, elaborately casual. She wanted to know if he still dated only tanned, long-stemmed, big-bosomed blondes, or if he ever varied the pattern, but she could hardly ask him that outright.

He looked down at her skeptically.

"If you think I believe that, Red, you're being even more naive than usual. By now I know you well enough to have discovered you *never* ask about anything without some underlying purpose."

"Curiosity, then," she offered.

"Try again," he advised, apparently not believing that was the reason.

Eden sifted hastily through her mind. "I'm doing follow-up research on the same survey I was conducting ten years ago." She tentatively said this, so that it sounded like a question.

Alex chuckled. "Okay. I give up. Keep your motives to yourself, whatever they are."

They walked without speaking for a while as they traveled along a rugged portion of the creek bank.

"I really do wonder what became of some of the girls I used to see you with," Eden said when the path smoothed a bit. "They were uniquely pretty, and I've sometimes wondered whether extraordinarily attractive women have an easier time coping with different phases of life than the ones who are more common in appearance."

"Probably they do, overall. At any rate, I imagine if they were given the option, most women would choose to be above rather than below average in looks."

"But don't you think beauty could become a handicap if it were excessive?" Eden theorized, deep in thought. "Peter Schuyler's mother was recognized as a great beauty in her day, and she once told me that she had a very difficult time adjusting to middle age because she suddenly discovered that she was invisible."

Alex shouted with laughter. "Well, that certainly is a terrible thing to have to contend with," he said judiciously.

Eden halted abruptly and glared at him with irritation. The effect was lost on him, as his back was to her.

"It isn't funny," she said indignantly. "I can understand what she meant by it."

"So explain it to me," Alex invited, looking back at her. His eyes still reflected his amusement.

"What I think she was referring to is simply that she'd been accustomed to turning heads wherever she went, to everyone admiring her. And gradually, as she grew older and her looks faded, this stopped happening. Nobody looked at her any longer; they looked around her, past her, through her, but not at her. Even"—she paused for emphasis—"even her husband didn't really look at her anymore."

"That's an interesting theory, Red." She could tell by his voice that he was still grinning. "Maybe it explains why some older women go overboard on cosmetics and prefer to wear such gaudy colors."

"Well, I think it's sad," Eden spoke heatedly, "that some people place so much value in something as superficial as physical characteristics."

"That sounded very much like an accusation," Alex remarked. He stopped walking and turned to study her. "Is that what it's all about—the interest in Monica, idle chatter about whether it's really detrimental to a woman to be striking, hints that possessing great beauty somehow prevents a woman from being loved for herself—all leading circuitously to the point that I prize certain feminine attributes too highly."

"If the shoe fits," Eden replied tritely.

He held some low-hanging branches aside and, stepping out of the way, allowed her to precede him on the final steep incline to the spring.

"Then you must also think I should be more appreciative of certain intangible qualities—a sharp tongue or mule-headed stubbornness, for instance."

She didn't reply but concentrated on finding secure foot- and handholds on the stony climb. Alex gave her a boost at one point, pushing her easily upward with one hand on her hip and the other on her waist, to a purchase that was beyond her reach.

"Do you think I don't enjoy looking at red hair, bewitching gray eyes, a saucy freckled nose, and a tantalizing little tush?" he asked softly.

For an instant she was riveted by the question, then she presented her back to him as she reached above her for the next stepping-stone, causing her jeans to tighten revealingly about her hips and thighs.

"The view from down here is *fan*tastic!" The comment was followed by a shrill wolf whistle.

He's only teasing me, she thought, but she was more breathless than was warranted by their hike.

She began moving rapidly upward again, eager to reach their destination.

"Maybe you think I should demonstrate my appreciation of your charms more appropriately," he persisted maddeningly. "Is that what's bugging you? Are you disappointed because I haven't made another pass? If that's the case, I'd advise you to grow up. Lovemaking that doesn't go beyond petting isn't fun —it's only frustrating—and I gave it up long ago!"

His tone was icy now, and she knew he wasn't teasing her at all. Would she never learn that she inevitably ended up the loser if she tried to match wits with him? She was rescued from the necessity of a reply when the spring came into view and Alex stalked by her.

The end of the pipe was correctly submerged in the spring, but when he looked down at it through the clear, cold water, his expression hardened.

"Dammit!" he groaned. He leaned down to examine it more closely and muttered another oath.

"What's wrong, Alex?"

"Parkins! That good-for-nothing bastard must have removed the screen from the mouth of the pipe."

He shifted the end of the pipe to show her.

"Hell! The pipeline might be plugged anywhere in the entire half mile of it."

Silently fuming, Alex worked for some time, digging debris out of the pipe, even uncoupling the first section from the next one. When he saw that that section was also occluded, he straightened and said disgustedly, "Damn! I should have foreseen that Parkins would pull a stunt like this."

He glanced at Eden as she sat on a fallen log at the side of the spring, quietly watching his efforts to clear the line.

"Sorry, Red," he shrugged. "It looks as though we won't have running water for the rest of the summer. We'll have to carry water for cooking and drinking, and bathe and do our laundry in the lake."

"It's only two weeks," she said, smiling to show it didn't matter that much. "We'll survive."

# Chapter Ten

Being without running water turned out to be more of a problem than Eden had visualized, especially when the weather, without warning, turned sharply colder, and the water in the lake developed an arctic chill. It seemed apparent that in the high country summer was over. During their last few days in the mountains, lacy crystals of frost rimed the windows in the mornings, lay in a thick white layer on the roof, and carpeted the deck.

Alex still swam in the lake while Eden watched, disbelieving, from the shore, shivering even at the idea of being enveloped in those icy depths.

"You must be part polar bear," she called to him one day while he was toweling off after his swim.

"You peeked!" Alex cried in a high falsetto as he struck a pose of false modesty, holding the towel in front of himself. Eden was reduced to helpless laughter as he chased her along the shore, threatening to throw her in the lake for her sins when he caught her.

Eden began carrying extra water to use for bathing, after obtaining a dispensation from Alex to heat it. Their remaining supply of bottled gas was more than adequate to provide for this luxury. Alex made a number of snide remarks about how she couldn't take it when the going got rough, but he generously took over the chore of transporting the extra water she required.

The fireplace provided their only source of heat, and in addition to the problem of carrying a daily supply of water from the lake to the cabin, they had to contend with just staying warm. Keeping the woodbox stocked took more time and labor than it had before.

It was fortunate that the windows facing the lake had a southwestern exposure, so the sun shone in and kept the temperature in the main room comfortable during the afternoons. When the sun sank behind the mountain, Eden wrapped herself in the warmth of the Navaho blanket, discovering it was practical as well as handsome. At night Alex put on a bulky knit sweater with a rolled collar but other than that, he made no concessions to the cold.

The final draft of Alex's book was finished on the day before their stay at the cabin was to end. He had been working to complete his editing like a man possessed in order to meet the deadline he'd agreed on with his publisher, and drove Eden as well. Late that afternoon Eden typed *The End,* removed the final page from the portable typewriter, and replaced the machine in its carrying case. She gathered up the neatly typed pages from the table in the kitchen and stored them in the box with the rest of the manuscript before she went out to the porch, where Alex was making minor repairs to the fishing reel. He looked up at her as she approached.

"Well?" he said, quizzically raising one eyebrow.

"I've finished," she replied.

"And—"

"Oh, Alex," she exclaimed, "it's a wonderful book!"

He gave a wild war whoop and jubilantly scooped her up in his arms and swung her around, again and again, until she was dizzy and had to cling to him to keep from falling when he finally put her down. She was laughing and breathless.

"You really like it?" he asked anxiously.

She nodded vigorous confirmation. "Someday when you're a famous author," she predicted, "I'll be able to tell people I knew you when you were an unknown."

"This calls for a celebration," he announced exuberantly. "We should have a party. I brought a bottle of champagne with me for just this occasion." He laughed. "It caused more than a few raised eyebrows when I added that item to the list of supplies to be packed in for us."

"I'll fix something special for dinner," Eden volunteered.

"*Anything but fish!*" they proclaimed in unison.

Eden giggled and quipped, "If I ever have to look at another trout, I'm afraid I'll grow fins and swim upstream."

"Trout don't swim upstream, salmon do," Alex corrected her, shamming severity.

"Well"—Eden was unoffended—"I never want to eat salmon again either!"

They parted company then. Alex took the magnum of champagne, submerged it in the lake to chill it, and carried in wood to fill the woodbox while Eden assembled a more than passable beef Stroganoff from their sadly depleted food stores.

They were both lighthearted when they met for dinner that night, their levity increasing as the level of the champagne in the bottle went down. Alex offered her her third cupful, waggling his eyebrows and faking a villainous ogle, as he melodramatically invited, "Have some Madeira, m'dear." Even as they ate the Stroganoff, they turned to a topic of conversation that had recently become a favorite with them— the foods they'd missed most during the summer.

"A thick, juicy steak . . . rare," Alex said.

"Or a hot fudge sundae with loads of whipped cream," Eden replied dreamily.

"Picture this," Alex mused. "A crisp green salad with mushrooms, garbanzo beans, tomatoes, artichoke hearts, avocado—"

"Stop," Eden groaned, "you're killing me!"

"Cold beer and pepperoni pizza—"

"Fresh milk—"

164

"A baked potato with *real* sour cream and chives —"

At last, satiated by their imaginary banquet, they became silently reflective while Alex refilled their cups with champagne once again. Eden had discovered she liked the taste of it, and happily accepted more of the sparkling wine.

"What are your plans now that your book is finished, Alex?" she asked when he'd rejoined her at the table. "Will you write another?"

"Eventually. The publisher might want some minor revisions on this one first though." He frowned into his champagne, deep in thought. "I'd like to continue my research with the Foundation too. If they decide to go ahead with the site in Eureka, I'd like to transfer there and make that my home base. My mother's health has been deteriorating, but I can't convince her to give up her home there and I'd like to be where I could keep a closer eye on her."

"Wouldn't a drier climate help her arthritis?"

"It might," Alex replied, looking up at her with a rueful smile. "It's just that she's committed to remaining in the house where she lived with my father."

"They were very happy together, weren't they?"

Eden drank her champagne to cover her wistful expression and didn't listen to his answer. *This is our last night,* she thought. *Tomorrow we'll close the cabin and hike out to the road, and Milton Graham will be waiting to drive us back to town. And when we get there, we'll say good-bye, and it will be all over. If we*

*both stay in the Eureka area, I may see Alex occasion-*
*ally, and he'll say, "Hello, how are you?" Then we'll*
*pass one another as if we were strangers, and he'll*
*never know how much I love him.*

*I was right about love, she told herself. It hurts—it*
*hurts terribly, and I haven't much joy to balance the*
*pain. If I could turn back the clock, go back to that*
*night on the top of the mountain, I'd make love with*
*Alex under the stars and not care if the sun never rose*
*again.*

"Are those tears, Red?"

Alex's voice interrupted her wishful thinking. Everything was blurred by her tears, and she hadn't
even realized she was weeping.

"Yes." She smiled at him and tried to sound as
effervescent as the wine, as though she hadn't a care
in the world.

"I'm crying for more champagne!" She held out
her cup.

"Maybe you've had enough," he declared. "I get
the impression you aren't used to drinking very
much."

"I don't usually like the taste, but this is very
nice."

"It ought to be, at the price I paid for it," he
grinned, "but you're not supposed to gulp it down
like that."

"I wasn't gulping," she denied, affronted by the
criticism. "I do not gulp."

She tried to rise so she could leave the kitchen in
a dignified manner but she seemed to be having diffi-

166

culty with her sense of equilibrium and sank into her chair again.

"All right," Alex said evenly. He looked amused. "I'll concede that you only gulp as much as you fidget."

"Fidget!" she shrieked, then composed herself and calmly stated, "I do not fidget." She glared at him.

"Next thing you'll try and tell me is that you're not tipsy."

"I am only as tipsy as I think I am," she responded, pleased by the neatness of the reply. "Tipsiness is a state of mind."

"Like happiness," he remarked, and asked softly, "Are you happy, Red?"

She greedily drank more champagne and didn't answer him. *How can I be happy,* she silently inquired, *when I love you?*

"They say part of achieving happiness is knowing when you've found it." He pursued the issue. "What would make you happy?"

She looked directly at Alex and scowled, trying to bring him into focus. Inexplicably there seemed to be two of him. She held out her cup again to the Alex on the left.

"I would like more champagne," she enunciated slowly and clearly. "That would make me very happy."

"At least no one can accuse you of asking for more than you deserve." He sounded exasperated, but she couldn't see his expression well enough to be sure that he actually was. "If you want more, come and get it," he said gruffly, as he stood and, picking up the champagne bottle, left the kitchen.

By using the table for support, Eden managed to reach the door to the main room. Alex was sitting on the couch near the fire, tuning his guitar. She'd have to cross a broad expanse of open space to reach him. She let go of the doorframe and stood there, swaying insecurely. She bit her lip and moved forward—one step, two.

The room spun crazily around her. *Oh, God,* she thought, *I'll never make it!*

"I can't," she cried. "I can't do it by myself."

Alex studied her coolly.

"Please, Alex," she implored him, "help me."

He put his guitar to one side and came toward her.

"It's about time you discovered you aren't entirely independent," he said irritably. "What is it you want my help with? Do you still want more to drink?"

"No." She shook her head emphatically, her eyes downcast. She felt that he was watching her intently. How could she brazenly tell him, "I want you"? Her lips moved to form the words, but they seemed to stick in her throat.

"Say it, Red," he prompted. "All summer I've wanted to hear you admit you can't make it alone."

She started to speak, but he continued, anticipating her argument.

"Oh, you'd accept my assistance willingly enough if it were offered, but you never once directly asked for it. Even when Parkins attacked you, you didn't cry out or call to me!"

168

She raised her eyes and their glances locked. All at once she was sober, and her mind was functioning with clarity and precision. Was the problem, then, simply that his masculine vanity needed to be salved? She thought of offering him the excuse—honest so far as it went—that she'd been unable to call for him because Parkins had kept his hand over her mouth, but she knew that, foolishly, it would never have occurred to her to scream. She couldn't bring herself to shade the truth about this. She'd concealed the truth from Alex for too long—almost until it was too late.

"Dammit, Red," he urged. "*Say* it!"

"I want *you,* Alex."

She whispered the admission and saw a glow of triumph leap into his eyes before he caught her in his arms and crushed her to him, so tightly, she could scarcely breathe. He held her without moving, without speaking, until they were both trembling with the overpowering force of their desire, until in the same instant they sought one another's lips and their mouths met and fused. The room seemed to swirl about her as he swept her up and carried her to her room and there, in the darkness, everything but the two of them faded away and became lost and unreal.

She clung to him and followed where he led as though she were a flower turning her face toward the sun. She was aware of her clothing falling away from her, of his hands learning the intimate secrets of her body and teaching them to her, of the rising urgency of their kisses, of the intensely exciting touch of him

—the feel of him. And still she craved for more, and her hunger became a sweet torment.

She didn't recognize her own voice in the hoarse, muffled cry that escaped her at the moment of exquisite pain she knew as he guided her through the mysteries of love. Tenderly he coaxed her to a passionate, almost frenzied, longing to know the ultimate mystery. Sweetly, skillfully, he created within her a pleasurable tension that grew and grew until it became very nearly unbearable.

"Eden!" Alex cried her name exultantly, as though rewarding her for waiting so patiently to hear him say it, and as one they reached the ecstatic peak. The awesome splendor of release was revealed to her—so blinding in its perfection that when she closed her eyes to savor its brilliance, she saw it still, and felt herself dissolving in the crucible of love.

"Eden," Alex murmured huskily against her ear, so softly, she might have imagined it as she lay in his arms, spent and replete with love for him.

"Making love to you is paradise," he whispered, and even as he spoke his fingers gently traced the wet streaks on her cheeks made by tears of joy.

She wanted to tell him that the consummation of her love for him was the most beautiful thing that had ever happened to her. She wanted to tell him that he was right, that the joy of it far outweighed the pain. But he was completely relaxed and sleeping deeply, with the warm weight of his body still sheltering hers, so she held him in her arms and surrendered instead to the tenderness of the moment.

He had not said he loved her or whether he wanted to continue with their marriage. But then, she admitted, neither had she. And perhaps the latter was for the best. If he didn't return her love, she would never burden him by confessing her feelings for him.

Her only remorse was for the fact that she had remained paralyzed with dread, poised with indecision on the brink of her love for him for most of the summer—when she should have taken the plunge with arms opened wide to embrace love fully. With her hesitation she'd only made her love for him appear complex, when in reality it was all so very simple.

But now she knew that whatever tomorrow might bring, she would never regret tonight.

## Chapter Eleven

Eden woke early the following morning and crept quietly out of bed. Alex was still sleeping, taking up most of the space in the small bunk. She moved carefully, getting into her dressing gown and collecting toilet articles and clothing.

She made some coffee and drank it while she waited for the water to heat for her bath. For a tub she used an old copper-plated boiler that Alex had found in the tool shed, and she dragged it out of the pantry, placing it in front of the cookstove, where it was warmer.

The day was a cold one, and the pale ball of the sun was suspended just above the ridgeline in the porcelain-hard blue of the sky. There were snow clouds massed about the summit of the mountain, but otherwise the sky was clear.

The basin was only large enough for her to stand in, and she filled it partially, reserving enough water for rinsing, then removed her robe and stepped in. She squeezed water from her sponge over her shoulders and breasts and soaped herself lavishly. Her body felt achy, tender, and unfamiliar to her, as though she'd been sensitized by Alex's lovemaking.

Alex came into the kitchen just as she finished toweling herself dry. Smiling and casual, he picked up her robe and held it for her to slip into. She was embarrassed by the intimacy of this service and kept her back to him, holding the towel around herself until she had the dressing gown on. Alex chuckled roguishly, amused by this display of modesty, and she blushed and averted her head to conceal the color that flamed in her cheeks, concentrating on tying the belt securely about her waist.

"Morning, Red," he said laconically. He wrapped her in his arms from behind, placed a kiss just beneath the delicate shell of her earlobe, and whispered, "Sorry I conked out on you last night. Too much champagne, I guess."

She stiffened in the warm circle of his arms.

"Then you don't remember—"

He chuckled again and contradicted her.

"Oh, I remember," he said emphatically. He nuzzled her ear again and added softly, "There was a full moon, and I ravished a maiden. It's just that after such a long lunar eclipse, once was not enough!"

He dropped his arms from about her waist and straightened slowly.

"God!" He winced and, placing a hand on his spine, he arched his back, stretching first to one side then the other. "That bed must have been constructed for midgets or contortionists."

"I'd better get dressed," Eden mumbled. This was not the way she'd imagined their first conversation after last night. It turned out she was a romantic after all.

Alex sighed. "That you had, Sunshine. Those are snow clouds out there, and we have a lot to do before we can leave." As though thinking aloud, he muttered, "I just hope the snow stays at the higher elevations till we're safely out of here."

It took all morning to put things to rights in the cabin and pack up the supplies that remained as well as their personal things. They stopped for a light lunch before they left, and it was nearing one o'clock when Alex finally padlocked the doors and they started up the trail away from the cabin.

They paused at the rise where they'd first seen it and turned back to look. Because it was an unusually cold day, frost still blanketed the roof, and the whiteness of it stood out sharply against the dark green of the pines. The few patches of the lake she could see were nearly the same jade-green as the trees and looked still and icy.

She felt close to tears and glanced obliquely at Alex to see if he, too, was saddened by their leaving, but instead of viewing the scene below, he was watching her. The chill wind gusted strongly about them, fanning her hair across her forehead and whipping a wild-rose color into her cheeks. His hands cupped them warmly, touched them gently. By contrast, his kiss was proprietorial: abrupt and hard, as though he were staking a claim. When he finally released her, she looked up at him, surprised.

"It's been quite a summer, Red," he said ambiguously. His voice was husky.

"Yes," she replied. "It was a good summer for me. I enjoyed our stay here, Alex."

"So did I," he agreed readily.

They began walking down the trail, their hands linked. He lifted hers and thoughtfully turned the wedding band on her finger.

"I captured a rare species of butterfly and found I'd gained a wife." Firmly he asserted, "You are my wife, Eden. There'll be no separation, no annulment, no divorce."

So it was settled, Eden thought. Her cup of joy was near to overflowing, and she could have skipped along the path with steps lightened by relief, but she continued walking sedately by his side.

"No comment?" he queried. "I can't believe you're at a loss for words." He squeezed her hand encouragingly.

"I—I'd like that too." She looked shyly up at him through her lashes. He was so strong, so steady, so handsome beside her.

"I guess that lukewarm response will have to do for now, Red. We'll talk about it later—tonight."

Tonight! As she thought of it her heart raced with anticipation. She would have a hot, scented bath and shampoo her hair. She'd have access to her cosmetics and perfume and she would wear her frilliest, sheerest, most alluring negligee, and he would see her looking feminine and pretty.

He grinned broadly with promise and said, "I have a king-size bed at home that should provide the ideal spot for our discussion." Could he read her mind? "I'm a great believer in body language," he teased, and was rewarded by another entrancing blush.

The hike out to the road was much less arduous than when they'd gone in. Not only was it mostly downhill, but Eden found her body was now conditioned to the thinner air of the mountains and to steep climbs and rough descents. She wasn't winded at all, and it was cool. In fact, as they pressed on, it turned even colder. Looking back, they could see the snow clouds locking the high country behind them in their icy grip. But Alex was no longer worried.

"At this altitude there's not much chance of an early blizzard," he told Eden. "Up where the cabin is though, it's another story. It's not very likely the snow will stick this early, but it could happen."

They saw no other hikers on the trail. It was too late in the year for most people. When they came to the stream Eden recalled as being so torrential, she was astonished to see how quiet, almost gentle, it had become now that the runoff from the snowpack no longer converged on it. With practiced ease, balancing lightly on the balls of her feet, she followed after Alex across the fallen log that bridged the gully. He'd had to help her when they'd crossed it before.

Alex had stopped on the far side to be sure she was having no difficulty at this point and seeing her proud expression at her accomplishment, he mimicked a drum roll and fanfare and applauded while she gathered imaginary skirts and curtsied as gracefully as though she were at a ball.

"That's my girl," he praised her, smiled, and ruffled her curls. His eyes said "tonight."

Milton Graham was waiting anxiously in the parking area at the end of the gravel road that terminated at the entry to the wilderness. He was a small brown gnome of a man who moved with birdlike quickness. He had a sprightly, Charlie Chaplin mustache and an unexpected gravelly bass voice.

"Hello, you two." He hailed them with the volume and tone of a foghorn. He and Alex shook hands and he clapped Alex on the back. He hugged Eden and kissed her cheek with affectionate warmth.

"You're both looking great, just great."

Their packs were stowed in the trunk of Milt's sedan, and they were off. It was only a little after six o'clock but it was already dusky, and the headlights carved a tunnel along the road through the trees as they bucketed along over the potholed road. They traveled at only thirty miles an hour but to Eden, after three months of traveling no faster than a run, it seemed as if they were flying. When they reached the blacktop and Milt speeded up to fifty, Eden closed her eyes, terrified, and gripped Alex's hand more tightly.

"What's wrong, Red?" he asked, concerned.

"It just seems so strange to be moving so quickly," she whispered.

"A little culture shock?" he suggested.

"A little."

"Think of dinner," he advised, "A steak—"

"A green salad," she contributed.

"And a baked potato," he finished. She smiled up at him, contented.

"This sounds familiar," Milt said. "We've found our returning couples' primary interest is in food."

"Oh," Alex drawled, "I wouldn't say that food is my *primary* interest."

"Well—ah—yes! Of course! I'd forgotten you two are newlyweds." Milt laughed uneasily and sounded disconcerted by his oversight, but he quickly recovered his aplomb. "How did you get along?" he asked. "Did you see many other people? Did you have any untoward problems?"

Alex began his preliminary report on the summer by telling Milt about their experience with Sam Parkins, and for a time Eden listened to the soothing drone of their voices.

She sat close to Alex with his arm stretched out along the top of the car seat behind her as he half turned to talk with Milt. In the somnolent warmth of the car her eyelids grew heavy, and she nodded from time to time until Alex moved his arm to encircle her shoulders and pressed her head against his chest. She relaxed against him as naturally as if she'd done this hundreds of times before and, sighing blissfully with happiness at being there, she stopped battling to remain awake and napped for a time.

They stopped for dinner in Redding. There were so many cars, buildings, people. The brightness of the fluorescent lighting in the ladies' room where she went to freshen up before they ate seemed alien.

She washed her face and hands and combed her hair with her pocket comb, studying her reflection in the mirror. Her hair had grown long enough to curl about her collar, and she'd lost her plucked-chicken look, but of course she'd known that. What was different about her was that her eyes were serene, sparkling, confident, and her color was vivid even without artifice. Even her freckles seemed to have assumed a new attractiveness. She remembered looking in the mirror at Elaine's, at Annie's, and again on the first night at the cabin. Quite a difference, she told herself. Her life had taken on a new meaning, and she had a new purpose.

She joined the men in the dining room. Milt had ordered champagne, and Alex exchanged a warmly reminiscent glance with her as Milt proposed a toast to their continued happiness together, to the success of their summer.

Over dinner, talk turned to what had been happening in the outside world since their isolation had begun. The international news was as depressing as ever, the political news as uninspiring, the cost of living was still skyrocketing, the baseball season was winding down, and the football season was getting under way.

Eden felt so fundamentally altered by her experiences of the past three months, she was slightly perturbed to learn that everything else had remained essentially unchanged.

The cocktail waitress who served Alex and Milt their after-dinner drinks was a stunning blonde whose skimpy barmaid costume made the most of her figure. She flirted openly with Alex, and when she served him, she leaned over in such a way as to display a close to indecent amount of cleavage.

Alex seemed to be enjoying it all. Eden was rankled by his undisguised interest in the blonde and decided he was doubtless flattered by the fact that she was attracted to him. Her newfound confidence in her own appearance evaporated as the lighthearted banter between Alex and the girl continued until she felt like a deflated balloon—and about as appealing.

Much as she enjoyed her meal, she was glad to leave the restaurant and resume the journey. She felt she could hardly wait until they arrived at home in Eureka.

They were nearing Weaverville when Milt's car developed mechanical problems. The car was a nearly new Buick, and he couldn't understand why it should be overheating, but it was. He pulled into a turnout at the side of the highway, and he and Alex each tried tinkering with the motor for a time before Milt said dejectedly, "We'll never find anyone to repair it at this hour of the night."

Alex made some consoling comments, but Milt

remained unencouraged until suddenly he brightened.

"I have some friends who live near Weaverville. You remember the Olivers, don't you, Alex? They'll put us up for the night."

Alex readily agreed to Milt's proposal that they stay overnight, have the car repaired in the morning, and then continue on to Eureka.

As it turned out, Joe and Nancy Oliver were a kindly, gregarious, middle-aged couple who greeted them as effusively as if they'd been invited guests. Nancy was a nonstop talker, and after the exchange of introductions and greetings was completed, in the time it took her to show Eden to the bathroom, Eden learned the names, ages, and occupations of their two sons, the foibles of their daughters-in-law, and the virtues of their grandchildren.

"We get a little lonely here," Nancy revealed pathetically. She actually followed Eden into the bathroom and sat on the commode while Eden bathed. "We used to come here for summer vacations when our boys were teen-agers and we liked it so much that when Joe retired, we decided to make this our permanent home. The problem is, we've both lived in big cities most of our lives and, stuck out here in the sticks as we are, we miss having neighbors all around us."

She provided one of her own nightgowns for Eden to wear—a full-length, long-sleeved, high-necked, shapeless sack that was several sizes too large for

Eden's slight figure. "My goodness," Nancy laughed, "you are a little thing, aren't you."

Eden's spirits plummeted when she saw herself in it, for she was swallowed by its voluminous folds, but she concealed this from Nancy behind a facade of gratitude.

*It isn't her fault,* Eden thought, *that tonight is turning out so differently from the way I fancied it would be.*

Still, in spite of the lack of privacy, she enjoyed the luxury of her bath. She washed her hair and while she filed the short halfmoons of her nails to smoothness and buffed them, Nancy brought out her hair dryer and dried it for her, exclaiming over what a glorious color it was.

She rattled on and on and eventually Eden began filtering out most of what she said and listening only in snatches, as if Nancy were broadcasting on a frequency whose reception grew alternately stronger and weaker.

"Alex is such a handsome man, and charming too! You're very lucky to have him for a husband." That came in loud and clear. "I remember when we were in Santa Barbara, he always seemed to have the most beautiful girls trailing after him."

*So I've noticed,* Eden thought ruefully.

And she heard: "I don't know how you could stand being way off in the mountains by yourselves all that time."

*As you recently pointed out,* Eden replied with silent reason—since Nancy hardly paused to draw

breath, let alone give her the chance to participate—
*my husband is a handsome, charming man.*

Her ears grew increasingly weary of Nancy's
voice. "I suppose," she told herself, "I'm just not
used to all this talking going on." It wasn't that Alex
and she hadn't conversed, but neither of them had
ever descended to an uninterrupted, essentially uncommunicative monologue either.

Alex knocked at the door of Nancy and Joe's bedroom shortly after that, and in her eagerness to see
him Eden forgot about the Mother Hubbard she
wore.

"Is my wife in there, Nance?" he called. "It's late
and we want to get an early start tomorrow."

"Come in, Alex." Nancy laughed heartily. "Eden
and I were just having the nicest chat."

"I can imagine," he said as he came into the room.
His eyes were bright with suppressed laughter, for he
was acquainted with Nancy Oliver's proclivity for
talking. Then he saw Eden as she stood just behind
Nancy and he sobered; his eyes widened as he surveyed her.

Her fingers tightened about the hairbrush she held
and she thought, *If he says one thing about this nightgown—just one thing—I'll throw this at him.*

"I'll show you to your room," Nancy offered, and
started down the hall with them trailing behind. The
bungalow was not very large, and their bedroom was
only two doors down from the Olivers'. Nancy
paused in front of the doorway uncertainly.

"I should apologize for the room," she remarked

before she began to explain. "Our sons shared it when they were home—"

"I'm sure it's very nice, Nance," Alex cut in, "and Eden and I are just grateful for your hospitality."

"Yes," Nancy agreed, still doubtful. "Well, good night," she bade them. "Sleep well."

"Good night," they chorused.

They watched Nancy's plump retreating back until she reentered her own room.

"God," Alex exclaimed, "it's been a long day."

He'd showered, Eden noticed, and somehow he contrived a devastating, virile attractiveness even in a borrowed dressing gown that was much too small for his broad shoulders. He smelled faintly of lime and mostly of himself—a clean, warm, masculine sort of scent. He opened the door and turned on the overhead lights with the wall switch as they entered the room.

Eden's face fell with disappointment when she saw the bunk beds with which the room was furnished. Her glance skidded quickly away from the beds and took in the rest of the youthfully faddish decorations in the room—the psychedelic posters and black lights, the beanbag chairs, the beaded draperies at the windows, the plaques of the zodiac symbols that described a huge circle on the ceiling—before her eyes sought Alex's face. He was obviously stunned.

"Well, I'll be—" He muttered an oath.

It was the last straw. Eden burst into tears.

"Red, honey, what's wrong?" She was crying with

**184**

hoarse, gasping sobs that shook her whole body. "It's not all that bad, is it?" Alex looked nonplussed.

She gulped and shook her head. How could she ever hope to explain?

He put his arm about her waist and guided her to a beanbag chair, collapsing into it and pulling her down with him onto his lap. She hid her face against his chest and he patted her shoulder and smoothed her hair, murmuring small endearments until her sobs became more controlled.

"What's it all about, Red?" he asked quietly. "Tears? From the same adaptable young woman who survived three months of hardship without complaint?"

"It was no hardship," she exclaimed heatedly, as if he'd insulted her.

"I'm glad you feel that way." He smiled tenderly at her, tilted her face to his, and kissed her softly on the lips. "But why let this upset you?" A wave of his hand indicated the room. "It's only for one night."

"It's just—" Her eyes fell away from his penetrating gaze and she fixed them on the gaping lapels of his dressing gown, on the dark, curly hair on his chest, and blurted, "The blonde, the beds, and this nightgown!"

He glanced at the ceiling and lamented, "Now there's a record-breaking combination." He tilted her chin again, forcing her to face him. "I understand about the beds, but what blonde?" His expression was puzzled.

"The one at the restaurant! She was—well, she had

such—and you—" She shook her head and gave it up as a hopeless task.

"One thing I love about you," Alex revealed, "is your enchantingly convoluted logic, but you're not usually incoherent."

He wasn't smiling or joking and he'd said there was something about her he loved.

"See if you can explain more lucidly about the nightgown," he directed patiently.

"I thought," she began hesitantly, "I'd wear something really feminine and sexy tonight, not service-able flannel pajamas, or durable jeans or—or this!" Her fingers plucked nervously at the high neck of the gown. "And I'd planned to smell of French perfume instead of Castile soap. I saw the way you looked when you saw me in this. You think I look a sight!"

He held her even closer, and she was pacified by this demonstration of affection even before he spoke.

"You don't need to worry about nightgowns or perfume. You're plenty womanly and sexy enough without trying to be. And you certainly don't need to worry about competing with blondes!" He tested a bright tendril of her hair between his fingertips. "Don't you realize how lovely your hair is?" He sounded incredulous. "It's another thing I love about you." He marveled as he pressed the coppery tresses to his lips. "It's like fragrant, silky fire."

Suddenly he frowned. "Now," he said briskly, "where are we on your list of problems?"

"Your expression when you saw me in this nightgown," she prompted, reveling in his tender persuasiveness.

"Oh, yes." He smiled at the memory she'd evoked. "I looked the way I did when I first saw you in that because you look so incredibly young. You've always seemed mature beyond your years. Maybe because when I first knew you, you were ten going on thirty —so I've always thought of you as being older than you are. Tonight I was surprised to find I'd taken a child-bride."

He leered at her suggestively. "But if you're so averse to the damned nightgown, take it off! That's how I'd most like to see you, you know," he added thickly, "wearing nothing but a smile."

He got to his feet, lifted her up beside him, and began working hastily on the row of buttons and bows that fastened the front of the gown, intent on his purpose.

"I love you, Alex." She said it simply but her face was exalted.

He grinned at her. "I thought I'd have to do some serious arm-twisting before I'd ever hear you say that. Maybe I should credit the champagne you had with dinner. It seems to affect you like a truth serum."

"You were the one who cautioned me to think before I acted," she reminded him.

"And I lived to rue the day that I gave you that advice," he groaned meaningfully. "Have you any idea how worried I've been that the summer would end before I'd managed to overcome your fear of being married?"

The last bow came untied under his eager fingers and he deftly slipped the yoke of the gown off her shoulders. She heard the sharp intake of his breath as the nightgown slithered to the floor to lie in a heap at her feet. Emboldened by his expression of admiration, she stepped away from it. She smiled and looked toward the beds.

"Which bed do you prefer," she teased, "top or bottom?"

Alex laughed raggedly and folded her in his arms. "Eden, I love you to distraction. Not only are you my wife, you're such a delightfully put together, sinfully desirable little wench that I don't know how I managed to keep my hands off you all summer and," he concluded in a soft tone, "there's a full moon again tonight—and every night from now on."

His hands began an exciting journey of rediscovery, traveling lightly, as though he were reading her body in Braille, over her back and waist and hips, then upward to the burgeoning fullness of her breasts.

"What does all that mean?" she asked breathlessly. Fluttering her eyelashes at him, she feigned innocence until she gasped under his knowing touch. She wrapped her arms around his neck and, rising onto her tiptoes, raised her mouth for his kiss.

His voice vibrated against her skin as his lips blazed a rapturous trail to search out the sensitive hollows of her throat. She seemed to be set alight wherever he touched her.

"Just that all day I've been waiting for the moment when I could make love to you," he growled softly, seductively. "So in answer to your question about which bed I prefer, *I* get the top, but we'll *both* take the bottom!"

**LOOK FOR NEXT MONTH'S
CANDLELIGHT ECSTASY ROMANCES:**

# Love—the way you want it!

## *Candlelight Romances*

# Dell Bestsellers